PEOPLE LIKE FRANK

People Like Frank

and other stories from the edge of normal

JENN ASHTON

TIDEWATER
PRESS

Published by Tidewater Press
New Westminster, BC, Canada
www.tidewaterpress.ca

This is a work of fiction. Names, characters, business, events and incidents are the products of the author's imagination. Any resemblance to actual persons, living or dead, or actual events is purely coincidental.

ISBN 978-1-7770101-6-4 (paperback)
ISBN 978-1-7770101-7-1(html)

LIBRARY AND ARCHIVES CANADA CATALOGUING IN PUBLICATION
Title: People like Frank : and other stories from the edge of normal / Jenn Ashton.
Names: Ashton, Jenn, 1963- author.
Identifiers: Canadiana (print) 20200283669 | Canadiana (ebook) 20200283707 |
ISBN 9781777010164
(softcover) | ISBN 9781777010171 (HTML)
Classification: LCC PS8601.S52 P46 2020 | DDC C813/.6—dc23

"Still" – First published in *Nunum*, Spring 2020
"The Bag and I" – First published on funnypearls.com
"Sundown" – First published under the title "We" on everydayfiction.com

Illustrations from original artworks by Jenn Ashton.
Cover painting: Norway, by Jenn Ashton, Lions Gate Hospital Collection

Printed in Canada

This book is dedicated to the many people I have known,
individuals who face barriers imposed
from within and without.
I have tried to honor your courage and
resilience in these stories.

STORIES FROM THE EDGE OF NORMAL

Nest

At 3:00 p.m. Betty put down her knitting needles and died. It wasn't 3:00 p.m. everywhere, of course, but in her own small apartment over the smoke shop it was. Betty had been knitting little bird nests for the wildlife and bird rescue center across town. There was always a call for them in the spring, when people would bring in eggs they found or when rescued mother birds could not find natural nest-making supplies within their man-made wooden chicken coops. Sadly, Betty's demise meant they would not be delivered. When people finally got around to packing up her place to make way for the smoke shop renovations, which would include her apartment being converted into a 'cigar lounge', the little knitted bird nests were fodder for the Goodwill bag along with most of Betty's possessions.

Francine McNamara was good at her job. She was good, and she was thorough, and even Steven her boss thought it but never told her so. He was twenty-three and believed that workers should do their best job and not be reliant on praise from their superiors. He'd seen that idea in a movie and adopted it as his own.

After her lunch break, from which she always came back

early—wanting to be the first to get started—Francine spied a bit of blue wool sticking out of the corner of an old cardboard box. It was near the door, in the pile that had been dropped off that morning. That was the other reason Francine came back from lunch early: she liked to make discoveries. She enjoyed the Christmas morning feeling of opening a box with no idea what was inside of it, like it was a gift just for her. Sometimes, when she was alone, she would silently mouth the words "thank you," as if the giver was in the room as she pulled out an old car coat or a pink-haired troll doll. Of course, she knew she could not keep these things, but she felt that she was giving them the love and respect they deserved, having been abandoned for whatever reason in the Goodwill's back alley. Francine knew a bit about abandonment.

She walked over to the box, which was surrounded by a mound of black, large-sized trash bags, which she knew would be full of clothes in various states of repair, bedding, drapes and paperback books. It was almost always the case, but the bit of blue wool held her attention and she reached over and claimed the box that had GOODWILL scrawled across its side in black marker. She took it to her sorting station, which was a green-legged stool and a long table by the back wall. She liked the back wall for a number of reasons; she could lean on it when she got a little tired, and the back wall was where the shelf with the radio was, and Francine loved to listen to the radio, especially the oldies station.

She heaved the box up onto her table and put on her blue rubber gloves. Chuck Berry was playing. Beside her was a large trash can for obvious garbage, and a few different colored bins, one labeled FOR CLEANING, one CLEAN, another MENDING, and one for QUESTIONABLE ITEMS. Questionable items were things that she needed to ask Steven about.

Francine carefully cut through the one piece of wide packing tape that helped the top stay shut and then she closed her eyes, took a breath and welcomed her gift. First she saw some large cotton housedresses—multi-flowered, but all clean, just out of a drawer, so into the "Clean" bin they went. There were some pantyhose and a few odd socks that had all seen better days; they went into the trash, as did old underwear (always). There was an old copy of *The Joy of Cooking*, a coffee mug, partially wrapped in a red tea towel, with some orange butterflies and "Betty" written in flowery script, and a small plastic bun bag, from which the blue wool was peaking.

Francine put the plastic bag on her table and finished emptying the box, flattened it, took it over to the skid where the cardboard recycling went and looked around for Steven. She didn't want to be interrupted.

Back on her stool, Francine carefully opened the bag. It was an old Kaiser roll bag and she could still smell the sesame seeds and bread. It smelled homey and welcoming, so she slowly reached in with her gloved hand. Francine knew better than to do it this way—they were supposed to dump out the contents of any bag onto their tables in case something sharp was inside. She knew better, but she did it this way anyway, she wasn't thinking too much about sharp things. She had that Christmas morning feeling and she was excited to see what she would get.

Her fingers didn't feel anything sharp, just slightly pointy and cold and woolly. She pulled out a ball of blue wool, some funny looking knitted things and a pair of silvery grey knitting needles—Size 2 it said at the top of each—with a just-started project attached and connected to the blue ball. She put the needles with the unfinished knitting to one side and inspected the other, rather odd-looking finished things. They looked like little, flat, round blue hats. Francine set one on her head and then immediately grabbed it off and looked around, hoping nobody had seen her. They weren't supposed to try things on. There were four of these knitted things, all blue, and each was about five inches across. She tried to think about what they could be: bowl? hat? fake breast? (she had seen those come through before, although they were made of rubbery stuff and not wool), knee warmer? some sort of game?

She continued to turn it over in her mind all afternoon as she worked, and then at the end of the day, she put everything back into the bun bag and put it on the shelf under her table. She was not finished with this mystery yet.

Back at home, Francine's evening routine never changed much. She felt safe in her routine, always knowing what would happen next. She saved her surprises for work. Easier on the system she thought, knowing you could rest at home, no sudden jolts.

The happy sameness consisted of taking the Number 12 bus from work to the group home. Even though she didn't like the words 'group home' that's what it was called. She liked to think of it as just home. She had lived there most of her adult life and never thought about living anywhere else. The people were kind and friendly, and the staff were helpful if you couldn't quite figure something out, like daylight savings time and how to change your clock back or figuring out how to allocate your money when prices kept rising, especially for bus passes and shoes.

It was the second Thursday so that meant that Susan was making dinner and Francine was on clear up. Susan always made a chicken pie with a crust that was so good that, sometimes after supper, Francine would sneak and break off some of the crust around the leftover pie and savor it alone in the kitchen. Its buttery goodness melted in her mouth and she thought life could not possibly be better.

After her chores were finished and the dishes were dried and set back into their cupboards, ready for the next day, Francine worked on her puzzle until 9:00 p.m. and then she began her bedtime routine. Pills first, handed out by Sandy the sleepover staff, then face and teeth. After that, it was laying out clothes for work the next day and crossing out this day on her cat calendar with the black grease pencil she kept on her dresser for just this task.

Francine always slept well, and her meds kept her from dreaming too much, so she always woke up the same, happy to start her new day. All these days were much the same, but the staff and the seasons changed, and celebrations came and went, but mostly it was the sameness that kept her grounded. She loved living her quiet life.

At 7:30 Friday morning, Francine's alarm clock woke her with the radio quietly playing Patsy Kline. It was a nice way to wake up and although she was happy, Francine also found herself a bit bothered that she hadn't figured out what the little knitted pieces in the bun bag were. It weighed on her and she didn't like that sort of itch in her mind, tugging at her thoughts while she went about her morning routine. Teeth, face, knitted things, hair, toilet, dress, knitted things, breakfast, bus, knitted things.

It weighed on her mind all the way to work, and even the bus driver noticed her frown and mentioned it, saying she should turn it upside down or something. She didn't quite understand what he meant and was too absorbed to think about it presently.

Once inside the door at the Goodwill, she wrote her name in the sign-in book and said hello to the few other people who had arrived, put on her orange apron and walked quickly over to her station and reached down for the bun bag. She checked the clock on the wall to make sure she had a few minutes of free time and then dumped the contents of the bag on her table and gently put each piece in a row to study them more closely.

The four things were all same size and probably the same number of stitches. She was guessing now—she didn't know anything about knitting or how to do it, a mystery for another time perhaps. Then the ball of wool and the few stitches that were on the needles, four on one and six on the other with a few wraps of blue wool around them to hold them side by side and then the blue ball. She carefully stuck the blue ball onto the needles, so they would stay neatly together while she worked on this puzzle.

At 8:25, May, who worked at the next station over, came in. May always smelled a bit like fish. With a few minutes to spare before they began their day, Francine asked May what she thought of the four round knitted pieces. May shrugged and walked on to her station, tying her orange apron behind her.

At 8:30, Steven came in and said it was time to start the day. So away went the bun bag back to its place under Francine's table and her workday began.

Saturday was library day at the group home and Francine was anxious. She knew exactly what kind of book she wanted today; it wasn't cats or animals of any kind, and it wouldn't be one of the Nancy Drew mysteries that she loved. It was going to be a book about knitting. She was determined to solve her own mystery.

The librarians were always very kind and patient, and Francine was happy to see Stephanie working today. She marched right up to her with her request, and the next thing Stephanie had surrounded her with knitting books on a large table. Francine didn't know where to begin. She had that Christmas morning feeling again, as she gently opened each book to peer inside. One by one she opened them and flipped through the pages but couldn't find anything like the contents of the Kaiser roll bag. Some of the books showed how to knit circles, but not her funny-shaped blue bowl circles. Stephanie brought one more book over. It was called *Archive: The Unfinished Ones*, and it was from Norway and filled with so many things to look at that Francine decided this would be the book she would sign out.

Back at home, she spent the rest of the day looking through the book. She did not understand much of what was written, especially the big black numbers under each photograph:

"0053 18.01.07." She thought maybe it was a code not meant for her, so she left it alone and continued to study the pictures. The book called them UFOs—unfinished knitting objects—and she was thrilled over and over again when she looked at each piece, even though none matched what was in the bun bag.

That night, before she got into bed, Francine sat down to have a think. Her meds were making her a bit sleepy, but she could clearly see the puzzle pieces in her mind. She thought that the contents of the bun bag should make their way to the Knitting Museum in Norway. Yes. Once she had felt those pieces snap together, she felt the uncomfortable tugging on her brain stop and she crawled into bed and fell into her customary solid sleep.

On Sunday, Francine was happy that Shelly was the person on duty because she was really helpful when it came to difficult questions, and the one Francine had woken up to was: how to remove the Kaiser roll bag from the Goodwill. She knew she was not allowed to take anything herself, and she wasn't sure she would have enough money to buy the contents of the bun bag, so she approached Shelly while she was peeling potatoes for supper.

Talking to Shelly about her mystery helped Francine make the decision to ask Steven if he would consider donating the Kaiser roll bag to the Norwegian Knitting Museum. She would show him the library book. Francine knew she would need to be very careful with it and take it to work in her backpack. She got little prickles up her neck and went a bit blotchy with nerves when she thought of approaching Steven with her request. Shelly role-played it with her until she was finished with her potatoes, and by then Francine was starting to feel quite confident.

So after one more sleep, she woke up on Monday morning excited to be taking the book to work to show Steven and maybe even May if she was interested. She carefully wrapped it in one of her pillowcases, so it wouldn't get damaged, and then slid it into her backpack. She felt like she had a special secret on the bus that morning and the bus driver remarked what a lovely bright smile she had today.

At work, she went and sat on her stool right away and waited for Steven with the book in one hand and the bun bag in the other. May gave her a funny look when she walked in, but Francine barely noticed, she was staring so hard at the door to the office. Then at 8:30 on the nose, Steven emerged from the doorway and said to start work. But instead of working, Francine bravely walked over to him and asked if she could have a minute of his time.

Steven was a bit taken back. Nobody ever asked to speak with him, and it made him a bit nervous, but still, he ushered Francine into his office and into a small chair at the front of his desk. He moved to his own chair and felt the safety of the desk between them. Steven put his arms on the desk, just to feel its solidity, and he asked Francine to proceed.

Steven knew he was fidgeting as she spoke, but he didn't know where exactly to put his hands or his head, so he ended up resting his head on his clenched fists. It seemed about right.

Francine was so caught up in her speech that she did not notice how awkward Steven was. Her eyes were on the Kaiser roll bag and the book, looking from one to the other as she explained her story.

Steven was happy to pick up the book and leaf through it, and then empty the contents of the bun bag onto his desk. He touched each item. The knitting needles he picked up for closer inspection, reading the number on the ends. Next the woolen disks, which he turned over in his hands, smelling the wool. Suddenly wanting to experience the texture, he put them to his cheek for a moment before putting them back into the bag. Next, he flipped through the book pages, one more time. This was an important decision, and yes, he thought these items should be in a museum, for everybody to enjoy. He liked the color blue, and the feel of the knitting in his hands. It reminded him of the winter toque his mother had knitted for him, and the decision was made. Steven even offered to type a letter to the Knitting Museum that Francine could send along with the bun bag. It seemed like an official thing to do, and it would look good to his bosses, who were always encouraging him to try new things.

Francine felt light as she walked back to her desk, hugging the book and the bag to her chest. May did not seem interested and just humphed when the smiling Francine went back to her station, tucked the book back in her backpack and put her apron on. Steven and Francine had decided that the Kaiser roll bag should stay on the premises until the letter was ready, and then Francine could take them both together and prepare a package to put in the mail. All she needed to do now was find the address of the museum and Shelly had promised to help her with that when she was on duty next. Francine hummed along with the radio songs all day.

When Francine got home that afternoon, she checked the staff calendar and was happy to see that Shelly would be working on Thursday, so they could look up the address together. Even though it was still a few days away, there was a lot to do to keep busy. Once she had explained her project, the staff helped her to find some brown paper and a box that would fit the long needles. Greta and Mary from her floor and two of the night staff got together and made a jar to collect coins to help pay for the postage required for the bag's long journey. The jar itself was just an old peanut butter jar, the kind with the green lid, but Mary let everybody use her felt pens, the pack she got for Christmas, and they took turns making a letter on the label which read "Bun Trip" in bright colors. Everybody put something in, and even Mr. Dimt the group home supervisor put in four quarters, which hit the bottom of the jar with a clank. Esther, who was older than Francine and walked with a cane, put in a little note that said, "Have a safe journey." Francine thought Esther was the kindest of the residents; if you were sad she would pat your shoulder or your head and say, "It's alright deary," and she always made everybody feel better.

Thursday was an exciting day; Steven presented Francine with the typed letter and together they slipped it into the bun bag. Then they put that into another plastic shopping bag, for extra safety, and placed it in her backpack. Francine and Steven high-fived when the backpack was zipped up, which made May laugh.

After work at the home, Shelly had found the address and

18

together she and Francine made a label on the computer in the dining room and printed it out so Francine could glue it to the brown-paper-wrapped box. It was time to go to the post office. Everybody wanted to go, so they warmed up the big van and six eager people piled in behind Mr. Dimt for the drive to the post office. Once there Francine counted out the money, and they all took turns to tell a bit of the story to the postal worker, who said it sounded like a fantastic adventure. Everybody patted the box goodbye and they stood and watched it go into the sorting pile and get wheeled into the back room, where its journey would begin.

The drive back home was almost raucous, everybody was very excited by the events of the morning and in the small group there was laughter and lively discussion and Greta even made up a song about the 'voyage of the knitting'. When they arrived back home, they clambered out of the van and walked through the front gate a little straighter and puffed up, each proud of his or her part in the adventure. Cheeks were red with excitement and fresh air and everybody was smiling and talking fast, imagining what would happen next.

Exactly one month later, an envelope was waiting for Francine when she returned from work, postmarked Salhus, Norway. After dinner, when everybody was still seated around the table, she opened it. She held up a beautiful card with a picture of a pair of knitted mittens on the front. Inside, there was a kind note written in English by a lady named Ann, thanking Francine and Steven for their gift, and saying she hoped one day maybe they could come and visit the Knitting Museum. She explained that the fancy pattern on the mittens was a Norwegian Selbu.

Francine took the card to work the next day and, after she

showed the note to Steven, tacked it to the wall beside her sorting table for all to see. She and Steven didn't talk about making the trip—why would they go to Norway when they were happy in their lives here? As the colors faded in the card, so did the memory of the note and the museum.

Far away in Norway, the lady named Ann added Francine and Steven's gift to a display cabinet at the Knitting Museum. She carefully set out the needles with the unfinished work and its attached ball of wool on a shelf beside the four blue discs, and then gently placed a yellow knitted bird into each, once again making them nests for orphans.

The Bag and I

I'm currently playing a game with the garbage man. Well, currently and for about the past three months. It goes like this.

Me: put a recyclable frozen asparagus package in the recycle bin.

He: throw it out on the ground.

Me: pick it up off the ground and replace it in the recycle bin for the following week.

I didn't know I was playing this game until I dumbly picked up on the repetition, like when you realize in Grade 2 that those games the teacher was playing with you in Grade 1 were actually meant to teach you something and you go "aha!" and then think how naive you were back when you were six. It was like that.

My part of this game also includes me trying to decipher why he has chosen this particular frozen asparagus packaging, when often in our bin there are two, and not only asparagus but the same brand of frozen blueberries or mixed peppers. All the packaging is the same, and all the correct type for our local bins, to be picked up every week. I have looked it up, three separate times, plus called my mother, just to be sure.

In my writer's mind, I have come up with many scenarios: a) he is trying to draw my attention to a larger problem (for example, the plight of asparagus farmers or some other issue he feels strongly about); b) he wants me to notice him so that at some later date he will use it as an ice-breaker ("You don't know me but we have something in common, the asparagus package," and we'll have a laugh); or c) he has a bit of a screw loose and just really hates /loves that asparagus package and does not want to see it made into a park bench or shopping bags.

Next week I plan to stand by the gate and spy on the garbage man to see if I can judge the look on his face or his actions: does he stomp on the bag, shake his head at it, does he curse it as he chucks it into the road? Then I begin to ponder the man himself, if it is just one lone man. What about when he was sick or on holiday, did the substitute garbage man do it too? Was it something that maybe got passed down the line, like playing that telephone game as a kid, where you sweetly whisper something into your friend's ear and their shiny short hair tickles your lips and you tingle at the warmth of your own breath returned from their ear cupped in your hand, and she whispers what she hears into the next person's ear and then by the time you have gone down a line of giggling kids the last person says out loud what she thinks the original sentence was, "I like you!" from the original, "That truck is blue" sort of thing.

So perhaps one guy was going on holiday and he left a message for his substitute, or rather, he asked the friend of a friend to give the sub a message and maybe the message was, "Leave my gloves in the back," and maybe the sub was a bit deaf and by the time the message got to him, what he heard was "Don't pick up any asparagus bags." Ok, maybe I'm reaching, but you never know.

Anyway, I am a bit obsessed with it now, and a few weeks ago I accidentally slept in and my husband took the bins out and I felt like it was Christmas when I woke up. Did he take it? Did he leave it? I couldn't wait to find out! And there it was, hanging limply in my husband's hand and I kind of giggled, glad to know the game was still afoot.

On Monday morning at a quarter past seven, I put the bins out to the curb and ensure it is all done correctly. One blue bin, one grey glass bin, one yellow bag for paper, and on the other side of the drive, three large bear bins with clips, one for garbage and two for yard waste. I unclip them all and double-check to see if there is any garbage in the garbage bin, as we rarely have any and I only put it out every month or so. There is, so I leave it. I stand back and am satisfied. Then I do a quick scan up and down the street.

This is one of the only times that I see so many neighbors on our road, and they're all in their pajamas. It's early and the dawn is just breaking, but I can make them all out and, like me, they are half asleep and near to tottering with their big heavy bins. I also check for animals, but the coast is clear; it's still just February and the bears won't be back for nearly a month. Then out of the mist to my left, I can hear the familiar wheels of a heavy shopping cart coming down the road, and out of the night I see emerge the older lady who comes regularly on this day to gather the pop cans and wine bottles out of the neighborhood bins. I read somewhere that she has made enough money doing this to put her kid through college and donate $50,000 to the local SPCA. I always wave and say hello and if by chance I do have anything with a return deposit, I make sure it's extra clean and near the top of the bin for her.

Once I feel I have done my duty, I sneak back through the gate. Not sure why I am sneaking at this point, but I guess I feel I should get into character, and by character I mean a sleepy girl in dark green dancing polar bear pajama pants with her husband's too big wellies and a bright orange teddy bear coat, the one I had been saving up for two years, then bought on sale and given to myself as a present from my non-shopping husband two months ago for Christmas. I only ever wear it to take the garbage out, because I don't get out much, so this event is a big deal.

Now that the bins are out and I am as concealed as I can be in said coat, I position myself just inside the dip of the front door frame, where I can sort of see the blue bin, where the asparagus bag lies, hidden by a similar frozen blueberry wrapper, same company, same wrapper, but with huge blueberries on the front.

I don't wait long, as we have to have all our bins out between 7:00 and 7:30 a.m. At 7:35, the big blue recycling truck comes along and I can see the driver in the tall seat and another guy hanging onto the outside of the truck whose face is hidden by a ball cap. He's wearing dark green coveralls and an orange safety vest. He swings down off the truck and grabs the yellow bag with the cardboard and paper and dumps it into an opening on the side of the truck; same with the gray bin, which he tips into another opening and I can hear the cackle of the glass jam jars and a Limmi bottle fall into the truck. Then he grabs the blue box and my heart stops.

Without realizing it, I take two full steps out of my hiding place so I can see what he's doing straight on, and just as he lifts the blue bin up to tip it into the truck, just in mid-swing, there is a loud beeping noise and our porch light goes on, illuminating me in my big orange coat and my husband opens the door with a sleepy "wharyoudoingouthere?" I glance ahead just in time to see the driver's hat move a few inches in my direction and I scramble to the side of the house to inspect the yellow paint. I nod a few times touching the siding and say quite a bit more loudly than necessary, "Hmm, yes, maybe you're right" and then I hear the truck drive away.

"Oh, Roger!" I seethe under my breath, "I was trying to see if that was the guy!"

"What guy?" Roger's bed hair is starting to relax in the outside damp and he pushes it out of his eyes.

"Ugh, the garbage man who always leaves the asparagus bag!" I whine, but by then he has lost interest and is heading for the coffee pot.

The city where we live is pretty small and, judging by how relaxed all the workers are, there may not be a lot to do on any given day. And by that I mean, if we need the arborist to come and check a tree, he shows up either half asleep or stoned (I can't tell the difference), and if we need the roads guy, he also shows up looking very relaxed, as if we've just roused him from a snuggly nap somewhere in his office or car and his cheeks look damp and rosy like a toddler who has just woken up. That, and they all have a sort of cheery serenity about them like most of the seven dwarves and I start to wonder if the city hall looks sort of like the Keebler Elves tree. I tried to convince Roger that in the right light the arbo-rist even looked like he had pillow face, but he just smirked at me, like I was making this stuff up.

But my point is, our city is small, so when you email or call them, you get a result immediately or within a few hours at most. They are so customer-oriented and even have email responders for all of their departments, so you never feel like your mail has just gone off into the void. And if you connect to the wrong depart-ment, somebody always writes back right away, saying that they have redirected your mail to the correct department, and they even give you the person's name and number and say when they will get back to you.

In the eight years that we have been here, we have never had anything but over, above and beyond excellent service from the city and that is why this one rogue garbage man is such a huge mystery to me. He doesn't fit in. He's a bad egg and has a bad attitude. Or so I imagine. What right has he? I say fuming to myself as I wander out to put the bins away and walk into the middle of the road, blue bin in one hand and asparagus wrapper in the other, scanning up and down the street for the glint of anything else left on the road. But there is nothing there, save the crow hopping around a few doors down, picking up what is probably a bit of our neighbors John and Margie's food waste that has fallen out of their bin in between the street and the tip into the truck. What I can see, though, is the blue garbage truck down at the very end of the street, and I wonder if the garbage man is looking back at me.

I realize within a minute that I am caught out and the morning sun is starting to peek through the trees and I'm getting warm in my coat and flannel pajamas and people are starting to drive their kids to school, and they're pointing and looking at me, quite out of place in the light of day, so I head back in once I've put the asparagus wrapper back into the bin and replaced it in the little wooden shed with the bear lock on the outside of the door.

Now I'm moping, but instead of waiting for another week to go by, I decide to contact somebody at the City Hall to see if I can find anything out. With a bit of a spring in my step after getting dressed and washing my face, I google the city and scroll through the department contact numbers. Roger is up and bustling in the kitchen with his cereal and blueberries, diligently giving a frozen blueberry to each dog. I look at the blueberry bag and wonder if there are any differences at all to the asparagus bag, besides the picture. Roger catches me staring in his direction and he laughs and shakes his head.

The city's website has had a recent upgrade. I know, because I beta-tested it. It now has bright pops of color, a new font and everything is really easy to find. I click on a little blue box that says "Get your garbage schedule" which I know should take me to the correct department. I have been on this page before, and also the one that tells what they will pick up and what they won't, and where there is a long list of what exactly can and can't go into each bin and box. There is also a search engine, where you can type in whatever you have to toss, and a message will come up with the information: "A peach pit can go into your brown food waste bag, which can then be placed, on collection day, into your yard waste bin."

I was also on the site recently because of the bears. Somebody came up with the idea of allowing people to put food waste into their bins, which meant the immediate death of tens of garbage bears, because: a) people would not lock their bins; and b) they would leave them out overnight instead of getting up early in the morning to unlock the bins right before the garbage men came. It was disheartening, to say the least, to see that this service had been put into place before thinking about the consequences to our wildlife. But that is for another story. Suffice to say, I knew my way around the website by now.

I scroll around the page and I'm actually not even sure I know what I'm looking for. Where can I find out about the people behind the scenes? I suddenly realize that the blue recycling trucks are hired by the city and so, no, I won't find anything on this page, so I google Smithrite which is the name on the side of the trucks, the foot-tall script in worn-out white but still bold enough to recall.

I don't remember seeing a phone number, but I'm guessing I can find something.

I'm in stealth mode now, head down, a crick in my neck that I'm ignoring. Hours have gone by, and between pondering the garbage man, scrolling through the internet and thinking about bears, I realize it's lunchtime and Roger has already left to take the dogs for a walk.

The area where we live is a little place in between many roads. It could be said that everything here was near a highway, like we are just a little stop for people hopping on and off the roadway for whatever reason. We're also in the middle of a forest, which makes it the perfect place for dog walking and witnessing wildlife. Even though we are only minutes outside of a major metropolis (via highway), we've often had a family of raccoons or skunks nearby, including under our shed, regular bears on the bear-trail that runs alongside our house, and the odd bobcat, coyote, rat, Lyme tick and various large raptors, some big enough to pluck up a small cat or a dog the size of ours and wing them away to a treetop for a snack. It is not unheard of to walk in our forest and see the bones of this or that creature or fish high in the trees. I suddenly wonder if a raccoon might be involved in the bag mystery.

Now I'm studying legislation from 2014 whereby the person or homeowner is no longer responsible for paying the recycling fees, then transferred over to the producers of recyclable goods. I think I can recall the newspaper article about this at the time, but I don't recall seeing it reflected on our actual property tax bill. Not that this has anything to do with the asparagus bag caper, but now I have fallen deeply into the rabbit hole of city policy.

As I climb my way out, Roger has returned with the dogs and he has something white in his hand. It's the asparagus bag! "No," he says. It's a frozen mixed vegetable bag that he found in the next block.

"Where?" I'm excited by this discovery.

"On Hoskins, about halfway down the block, in the middle of the road." We turn the bag over and there is nothing special about it. It's been washed out and smells like plastic and Dawn, its previous owners had done their due diligence. And as Roger is unleashing the dogs and getting them a snack, I make up my mind.

"I'm going for a little walk around" and he laughs at what must be my Sherlock face, determined yet good-looking, as I trade my orange teddy coat for a slicker because it's started to rain.

I start by casing our entire block, and then take a turn onto Hoskins, which has already been searched, I then take another turn onto Hamilton and walk the entire length of the crescent and back again, but no bags in sight. As I turn the corner onto Clarke, I can see something white glistening up ahead. I break into a run, the likes of which must have been comical for anybody watching, like maybe I was timing myself sprinting or maybe I was running from something chasing me. Any of my neighbors peeking out of their curtains would have looked behind me thinking they might see a bear. But no, it was just me running toward a white something on the road. And it isn't just any something, as I came closer and catch my breath, I can see that what is shimmering in the light rain is indeed a plastic frozen vegetable bag, this time "Mexican Mix: Red and Green Peppers with Slivered Onions." Eureka! I hold it up in the air like it's an Oscar and it drips water into my eye.

I walk home triumphant and sure that I am on to something big, not even thinking about the drizzle that has turned into full rain and is soaking me.

The following week I am back at my early morning post, but

once the bins are out, in a last-minute decision I decide to change my position and wait outside the gate up against the house, behind the car. Even though it is quite light out at half past seven near the end of February, I am well hidden by the SUV but have a clear view. I am about fifteen feet away from the bin which contains the asparagus bag and the shiny clean pepper bag which I placed right on top.

At precisely 7:35 a.m., the blue truck rounds the corner. I can only hear it, though, as it comes towards our house, because I can't see over the top of the car and have to wait until it is pulled up right beside our curb before I have a full view of man and bin, together.

I watch him jump off the truck, then methodically go through the row: the yellow bag of paper and cardboard first, bin of glass next and then finally, once again, the moment I have been waiting for. I'm not sure I am even breathing when he grabs the blue bin, swings it up and tips it over into the truck. To my surprise, he doesn't even look at the contents. He couldn't care less, he-wasn't-even-looking-at-what-he-was-doing! I stand with my mouth hanging open. I am confused. What is going on? I step out from behind the car and surprise him while he still has the seemingly empty blue bin in his hand. The noise from the truck is really loud so he smiles, mouths "Hi" and nods at me. The next moment is sort of a slow-motion blur, like when you just wake up from a scrummy nap and for a split second you don't know where you are; that is the feeling of disbelief that comes over me as I watch the garbage truck start to pull away, and the garbage man, all in one move, throws down the bin, runs a step and hops up onto the truck. Then it happens. I see the asparagus bag tumbling and turning a few times, end over end, cartwheeling down the road, caught in some kind of current as the truck drives away.

And there we are, the bag and I, alone on the road. Again.

I tell Roger later that I had considered this scenario some time ago (I hadn't). I mean, you know, it's only logical that as the bag was the first thing put into the often damp bin, it probably just got stuck to the side or the bottom. Just as naturally, after the garbage man tossed the contents into the truck and then dumped the blue bin back on the drive, the bag remained. Where, like a limp piece of baloney, it stuck, and then gravity simply did its work and the bag could do nothing else but fall out onto the street, where I would meet it, again, week after week, until I realized my mistake.

Remembering Vincent Price

Chrissy Evers is a slut
Chrissy Evers knows too much!

T he way the Band-Aid peeled off so easily, you would have thought the wound had healed, but it was still deep and oozing and the unremitting rhyme played loudly in her head: when she was shaving her legs, buying underwear or just sitting in the hairdresser's chair. The voices would find her while she practiced those highly recommended self-care strategies she had worked out with her therapist.

Any kind of accomplishment—graduating, paying bills, folding laundry—was completed with the cadence of the chant forever in her ears, like when you spread ripe avocado on toast and a small piece falls off for you to find later. The bit that somehow gets itself into your hair or smeared on your pants—it just never really goes away even when the pit and peel are safely tucked away in the recycle bin. The crushing voices always came back, and Chrissy's slut status never fully disappeared, because memories don't; they just become intermittent. That rhyme was her heartbeat, both the label and the question that raged after it, and that was the part that hurt the most, because she could never understand what she knew too much about.

Sometimes Chrissy answered the voices, from the safety of Ativan's calming hug: "Maybe I am a slut, but I've had some damn good times." Her right brain counted the remembered encounters, re-watched them, back when she thought more was better. Back before she grew up and got righted and realized she was victim and prey and not actually in charge. Now, when Chrissy looked back, she could only see a row of streetlights whose dusky yellow glow just shone on all her mistakes, all tidily lined up along the street where she grew up.

Chrissy got stopped on the path back and forth to school almost every day. There was a group of boys who hung out on the stone wall at the north entrance to the path. Some sat on the wall, some stood and some were on their bikes, the ones with the high handlebars and banana seats that she loved and longed for. "Slut!" they called out. She didn't know what that word meant.

Sometimes, though, on her way to school, they weren't there, and it was such a joyous relief when she would come over the crest of the hill and look across the street to see the entrance to the path, empty. She always tried to leave her house early so she could: a) miss them; b) run her hand along the hedge and stop to touch the petals of the million pale pink springtime camellias that sat there waiting for her, right behind where the boys usually sat; and c) be alone in the school library.

The trail to the school was at the end of a cul-de-sac, and that was where the boys sat. It was as if they were the guardians of the entrance to learning, and for almost all of her seven years at that school, her route was a torturous one and she was afraid. In reality, it was just a quiet gravel path that ran beside a house and that, after about fifteen feet, turned into a woodland trail, soft with bark mulch underfoot, and cool and shady with rustling trees overhead. Another fifteen feet in and there was a fork: the right trail led to the school's street and the left trail to a street farther down that didn't matter.

School was okay. It was a bit of an experiment. It had the area's first female principal and instead of classrooms, there was a large open area, where all the classes were sectioned off by rolling blackboards. Recess and lunchtimes were when the boys came out again and called you names or tried to look up your skirt or pinch your bum.

"I see London, I see France, I see Chrissy's underpants!" they would chant as they ran around trying to flip up your skirt. In the late sixties and early seventies, the girls were only allowed to wear pants two days out of five. On pants days, Chrissy felt safe and powerful.

Once she brought a wrench to school, tucked into her knee sock, ready to bonk anybody who grabbed her. It kept falling out throughout the day, but she didn't think anybody saw it, although some of the kids left her alone after that.

On the way home, the boys were always there at the head of the trail when she came out of the woods. Her six-, seven-, eight-, nine-, ten- and eleven-year-old hearts pounded in her chest, but she was ready for: a) being laughed at; b) being called names; c) being chased; or (and this was rare) d) it was only one or two boys, her friends Scott or Trevor. Then, they would just say hi and she could relax and even hang around with them for a while. But if some of the older high school boys, their brothers, were with them, smoking, Chrissy would retreat and cross the school grounds to the back trail, the one they weren't supposed to take.

Chrissy was unsure why the boys picked on her. No one her

age lived on her street anymore, so she didn't have any friends to walk with, that might have been part of it, she was always alone and an easy target. A few blocks down there were girls her age, but they all got rides. There was one kid who lived near the top of her street, but he cut up frogs on garbage can lids and so he was mostly alone too.

On a trip back to the old neighborhood some twenty-five years later, Chrissy drove by her old house. She was trying hard to come to terms with her past. Her therapist had suggested that she visit some of the places from her childhood to try and heal her younger self. The trees and bushes had grown up around everything, and as one would expect when you come back to a place a foot and a half taller, everything in the street looked small. The trail to the school had become an alley, wide enough for cars, no more trees left. There was nowhere for mean boys to hide or chase, no shade, just a hot light and pavement. She sat in the car and assessed. She tried to replace this scene with the one from her memory, to see if it would help erase some pain. It did not. She did not feel healed. She just felt taller.

She drove the few more blocks and parked across the street from her old house. She dared herself to knock on the front door, feeling a kind of ancestral ownership of the house. The front door was no longer faded and peeling wood, but a bright and shiny prefabricated thing, painted Swedish-flag blue.

An older woman with a Swedish Crown braid twisted around her head like a halo, answered her knock and looked puzzled as she said hello.

Chrissy stuttered out: "I grew up here, my dad built this house" and then the nerves grabbed her and she could feel her heart race and she looked away and out towards the gardens. "It's so much tidier now," she smiled scanning the yard.

Perhaps the owner felt sorry for the strange, anxious woman standing before her; she opened the door wider and asked her visitor to come inside. The house had changed quite a bit in the two decades since Chrissy had lived within those walls. The windows in the living room were shaded by neat wooden blinds instead of the old-fashioned heavy gold brocade curtains that Chrissy's mother always complained about. Then they went through the small hall and into the kitchen, now so bright. This room had been one of Chrissy's least favorite places and so many evenings she had sat there alone, in the gloom with a plate of cold peas in front of her, memorizing the ugly wallpaper covered with drawings of spices and pepper grinders. The unfinished basement where the big freezer had been was now a room decorated in a distinctive Scandinavian minimalist style with a wooden sauna to one side, and the adjoining rumpus room with its well-stocked beer fridge was now a sparse and welcoming art studio, which received a green filtered light as the sun shone through a row of potted plants on the windowsill.

The main staircase was now thickly carpeted, and Chrissy wondered why nobody had thought of that in her time—she had slipped and fallen down those stairs more than once when they were shiny hardwood. Looking down from the top of the stairs the house seemed so tiny but, like the kitchen, was now bright and airy, painted a fresh white.

Merja (that was the owner's name) led the way down the hall and opened the door to the first bedroom on the left, Chrissy's old room. Now a guest room, it was so small, especially with two adults standing inside it. Chrissy walked to the window.

She recalled summer nights staring out to the forest and down at the neighbors who were from Johannesburg (Jozi they called it) and whose kids had never seen snow until their first winter here. They had a pool in their backyard and the kids, though younger than Chrissy, got to stay up to all hours playing loudly outside. From her window, Chrissy could see her parents in this neighbors' backyard with glasses in their hands. When she thought about it now, that had been the "party house" on the block, where every weekend a row of unfamiliar cars would sprout up out front of their houses, often staying there until the next morning.

Standing there at the window, a flash of memory came so strongly that Chrissy's hands started to shake, and she could feel prickly beads of sweat push through her skin and roll down her back. Her heartbeat sped up and she could feel it pounding in her chest. She had an uncomfortable feeling in her neck, which grew tight like when her mother would do up the top button of her winter coat. Chrissy looked four backyards up: there was a high fence there now, but there didn't use to be. Her eyes strained to see, but she was not sure what she was looking for.

Her gaze shifted back into this yard in front of her. There was a yellow playhouse, which was now surrounded by beautiful flowers and used as a tool shed. In the next yard, the party house's, the pool was no longer there and instead there was a long lush green lawn and the back of that lot had been cleared of its tall cedars and she could see now, all the way to the back fence.

The backyard of the next house was hidden by a dip in the landscape, but over the fence, the fourth house, was where her eyes went again and strained. There was a memory, but her mind couldn't grasp it. Chrissy could feel herself turn clammy as a panic attack started and she asked to use the bathroom and once safely inside she rummaged in her bag for an Ativan.

Chrissy's panic attacks would hit anywhere, anytime, usually heralded by that clammy feeling and a racing heart. This one cut a bright light through her brain and behind her eyes, showing the flashes of a picture, some pieces missing, others unclear. She thanked Merja, who didn't seem to notice the change in her, and left quickly, driving home as calmly as she could, and trying to stay alert on the road as the Ativan slowly calmed the muscles in her body.

A bout of vomiting flu followed the panic attack and for the next few days Chrissy didn't take the bus to the university, where she was an interim instructor, but stayed in bed, marking a few student papers when she could. Her dreams were bad, and when she was awake, something crept across the surface of her mind that felt old and moldy. Chrissy often woke with a headache and a sideways feeling in her brain that wasn't quite right, like something was trying hard to push over a wall. Like an old hand with yellow fingernails tugging at the arm of her sweater, not leaving her alone. On days like this, the Ativan was her backbone and she relied on it more than she knew she should.

Four days after the visit to her old house, Chrissy woke up to a memory of a small girl with perfectly cut bangs. The girl had been Chrissy's friend before elementary school, and they would play and collect popsicle sticks on the side of the road in the summer. Her mother's name was Agnes and she had flaming red hair, Christmas hair Chrissy called it in her child's mind. She liked to go to the girl's house for something to eat. Just about everywhere had better food than Chrissy's house, where nobody cared to shop and, as a result, she was one of the skinniest kids on the block. She remembered tasting her first Oreo at this playmate's house, where cookies and milk were normal. But the sweet memory turned sour: she remembered a room, a strange one in her friend's basement.

The girl had called it her dad's "office." Chrissy remembered how they would slowly open the door and stand in the center of the small room so they could look all around. The walls and even the ceiling were covered, every inch, by naked women in various poses. Later, Chrissy would learn they were *Playboy* centerfolds, meaning they came from the inside of the magazine, with staples through their navels, through their center.

She remembered knocking on her friend's door one day, and Agnes was standing there so tall and looking scary with her hair flaming, saying that her friend couldn't come out to play. Chrissy went back again later that day, and then every day afterward for a time, but she never saw her friend again. Then that house was dark and Chrissy rode her bike quickly by, without looking, whenever she had to pass it. Later, after they had brought the bus line up her street, the stop was directly across from the girl's house and Chrissy was forced to look at it as she waited for her bus. It made her feel distant and sick. The house was half-hidden by trees in the front and the windows are always dark, not even a porch light turned on.

In the mid-seventies, Chrissy and her family moved away. She was already a teenager and her life had begun, and the secrets of the past were put away with the contents of that house, into cardboard boxes and wooden moving crates.

But now, as a woman in her thirties, something was gnawing at her from inside those boxes down in that dark and lonesome childhood. She thought it was the trauma of the bullying in elementary school, the teasing from the bike boys at the trail, but that memory had not made the uncomfortable feeling inside of her like the window did. There was something about her old bedroom window. The thick yellow burlap curtains that perfectly matched the delicate daisy wallpaper, the curtains that would be blown by the north wind when her window was open to keep the small room fresh. And the bookshelf above her bed, where the books toppled on her one night after an earthquake that nobody believed, *Charlotte's Web* falling on her head and waking her out of a dead slumber.

"Point your bed's head north for the best sleep," Chrissy's grandfather said. And so in that house, that was the compass direction all of their beds followed.

Different childhood memories would make their way painfully into her head for no reason at all and Chrissy often wondered if it was this way for everybody, though she was never brave enough to ask. While shopping for shoes, she remembered a fight she had had with her mother, screaming because she was never allowed to stay up past her bedtime. She could close her eyes and see her dad holding a stubby brown beer bottle and laughing loudly, her mom holding a wine glass; with her closely cropped hair, she was easy to pick out of the crowd of seventies bouffant hairstyles. Chrissy could see the two neighbor boys running and laughing and screaming, playing chase up the back fence line and then—what was that? In the corner of her aching brain, she could see something else, somebody playing tennis, a serve over and over. But there had been no tennis courts behind any of their houses. Then it wasn't a tennis racket she saw, but something with a point, something sharper, going up and down. Up and down. The man with the goatee, carrying a small girl wearing a striped shirt and a cast on her arm. Chrissy could see it. Chrissy dropped the box of new shoes and ran to her car, not to escape the memory, but to find a safer place for it to emerge. She got into the car, not intending to drive yet, but out of habit; to feel some form of security, she did up her seatbelt. Click. And then instead of reaching for an Ativan, she held on tightly to the wheel. Ten and two. Breathe.

Flash. *The schoolyard. It's sports day and kids are at the kinder-garten early and playing on the new slide in the center of a new play area. Chrissy's friend is climbing up the slide's ladder, and then calling out.* "Watch this!"

The girl with the perfect bangs starts to slide down backward but halfway down she tries to flip around and falls the six feet or so to the fresh blacktop around the slide. She is curled into a ball on her side, sobbing and holding her arm, as a group of kids makes a circle around her.

Chrissy remembered feeling protective, remembered telling them not to touch her. She doesn't remember anybody else ever going down that slide after that.

After school that day, her friend's mom said she couldn't come out, that she was sleepy from the medication for her arm. Chrissy went home and read Pippi Longstocking instead.

The little girl didn't come back to school after that.

Flash. *Chrissy screams. From the garden at the noisy neighbor party house, wine glass in hand, Chrissy's mother looks up to her daughter's bedroom window and scowls, probably thinking the Chrissy is yelling at her, still in their fight about staying up late. Chrissy wants to go to her mother, to say what she has seen, but she dares not open her bedroom door. Stay safe, stay small. She closes the yellow curtains and retreats to her bed, pulls the covers over her head and thinks about books.*

Chrissy remembered hearing a story about a girl who witnessed a murder by her neighbor but forgot about it, then when she heard about the missing person years later, she recalled the incident and went to the police. The police dug up her neighbor's backyard and there were the bones, exactly where the girl had remembered it.

But something wasn't right. Was this a memory of a story, or a memory of a memory? An old movie plot? Chrissy's skin crawled with anxiety again, still, like something she had no control over was seeping out of her pores and she scratched at her arms in frustration. She took a leave from the university. Each night, she tried to stay awake as long as she could, afraid of the pictures that would come in her nightmares.

There is a particular feeling when you are sleeping in a trailer and somebody steps up and inside, and it feels like the whole world lurches and moves and tips to one side with the weight before it rights itself. This was the feeling she had every morning when she woke up after a long night. It took her hours to right her mind again. Chrissy knew she could not keep this up.

Dr. Peters, Roy, her physician, wrote out a repeat prescription for Ativan. He was familiar with her panic attacks, but he saw from her darting eyes that this was worse than usual. Kindly, he suggested that she do some research, spend time with the microfiche at the library. The work might help her to actualize her memory. But there was nothing about any disappearances in her area, she couldn't find anything about her neighborhood during that time at all. It had been a new development, high up a mountain and there were only old notes in district meeting minutes about building permits. The gnawing in her mind and the feeling of fingers scrabbling down her back continued to worsen.

Heather. The breakthrough came some weeks later, in the middle of another bad night. She remembered the girl's name. It was Heather. Heather-with-the-broken-arm, flame-haired Agnes, dad with the "office" and the goatee.

Flash. *Chrissy is at a birthday party for Heather at her house. The kitchen is in the front right corner of the house. They are talking about movies that they liked. When it's her turn, Chrissy tells them about a movie she saw on television,* The Last Man on Earth, *about living dead vampires. Just when she gets to the part when the man's daughter dies and comes back to life, Agnes stops her. "How are you allowed to watch those movies?" she asked through her squinty eyes.*

That night Chrissy dreamed of Heather and her broken arm and Vincent Price hammering a stake into the heart of a dog.

Her doctor told her it would be okay to talk to the police. Suddenly Chrissy's body was on fire, but it was a good feeling. A cleansing burn. Yes, she thought, it's the right thing to do. Her body knew it.

On a cloudy September morning, she was sitting in the local police station, reporting a historical crime, explaining to a sympathetic Constable Andrews that she was almost sure it was a crime and not a memory of something else she may have heard somewhere in her childhood, an urban legend. He assured Chrissy that they would look into all of it. His desk was large and she was about five feet away from him. Still, if he had looked hard enough, he would have seen the gooseflesh creeping down Chrissy's arms as she told her story.

Now she was sleeping again, after weeks of nights when she had been mostly awake, sleeping on and off for only three or four hours in between nightmares. But now it was for a solid eight, and she was back at the university. There was a strange weight off her, like she could take a deep breath with no dark cotton clogging her lungs. She hadn't had a panic attack in months. Like finally finishing a large puzzle, she could run her hands back over her smooth mind, remembering every line and piece. She felt happy and relieved, and light.

The police had dug up the backyard of that house, four backyards away from her old home on her old street; they found the small child's skeleton, the remains of a plaster cast and the remains of an adult woman. Records showed that Heather's father had committed suicide in his basement office, after telling people that Agnes had left him for another man and had packed her things and their daughter and taken off, no forwarding address.

The house had sat dark and empty, across from the new bus stop, in the middle of a probate war for years. Nobody had ever questioned where the man's wife and child were. They all assumed that they had moved away, were happy and didn't want to be found.

Back then, you could get lost . . . and found.

Chrissy stopped taking the Ativan.

The Instruction of Thomas Epperman

I f nobody has read *The Instruction of Thomas Epperman*, they will now, thought Isobel as she pulled the t-shirt over her head. It was not just any t-shirt, but one from the top of a stack sitting at the foot of her bed, all white, all with a little pocket on the outside of the right sleeve. The t-shirts were exactly the same but for one thing: the words on the front of each one were different.

Isobel grabbed her brush and pulled it through her hair a few times without looking into a mirror. Then she brushed her teeth in the same way. Grooming was not something you needed to see, she thought, and she rarely looked into any mirror unless there was something she needed to see; her own reflection did not generally fall into that category. Rather, Isobel Emerson thought of herself as the mirror, reflecting the words that she believed people should see, read and know.

That's why she invented the t-shirt book. She would leave it until a later date to come up with a more marketable name, as she hoped others would pick up the cause as well.

Having recently completed her Ph.D. thesis on the topic of twentieth-century advertising—*Billboards of Modernity: Blending Goals at the Intersection of Awareness and Industry*— which included things like graffiti, tattooing, lamppost/telephone pole notices, art and advertising on plywood boarding and the like. Isobel was now going to live her thesis and develop a new method of communication. She was going to be a human billboard, with a different line from a book on her t-shirt each day.

At the start of the campaign, she was teaching a class on media and wore her shirts to every class. And then after class each day she would either stand in the hall or someplace out of the weather. The sleeve pocket of her t-shirt was stuffed with cards she had hand-printed with the name of the book and the author, Henry Sinclair, along with her website address for more information. She had cut the cards from scrap cardboard, cereal boxes, torn paperback covers or anything else she could find in the recycling bin. She'd stayed up late into the night, risking writer's cramp, to make sure she had enough cards for the hours that she planned to be out. And then Isobel would just stand. Stand and not speak. She stood silently and even though many tried to speak to her, she would just slightly turn to them, offering her right arm and pocket sleeve cards, or when the cards were gone, she would just look down at the words on her shirt. She didn't want to interfere with the words, lest they lose their power.

The cards went quickly, and even though some students may not have followed through and looked up the book or author or website, they liked being a part of the "show," as many of them considered this work "performance art" and viewed Isobel as the performer. It would take some time and explanation through the media to be understood as the educational act that it was supposed to be. In the early days, smiles did not come naturally, but she learned how to perform the gesture because the majority of students wanted to have their photos taken with her. She learned that if she did not smile, but only looked down at the words on her shirt, most students would walk away, but she if she adjusted the shape of her mouth, this engagement would draw them in and they would take it the next step further. Isobel could see the change in website analytics once she began smiling or putting her arms around students in photos. This was part of her own education, and it solidified for her the idea that the students had to feel a part of the endeavor to become interested in the work. Although this was a well-known concept, Isobel felt successful when she could prove its veracity.

Initially, Isobel was misunderstood by the larger academic community on campus, many of whom assumed she was a theatre arts student. For some reason, that made people think less of her, even though she was not acting. Verbal communication was not easy for Isobel; "doing and showing" seemed more natural to her than lecturing, and she was good at it. The response of her peers showed her as well that her work required a fluidity and refinement and an evolution in her system, that without those first few successful links (a smile, a touch) in her chain, from viewer to T-shirt to website engagement, her project became static and the final measurement goal (book sales, website traffic) could not be reached. But she still resisted explaining herself and her project to her students and people in general; she bit her tongue, smiled and looked down at the words on her shirt. Every time.

It took one year of t-shirts to share just one third of *The Instruction of Thomas Epperman* with the students and staff of Moberly University. At the beginning of the second fall semester, a student journalist wrote a profile of her for the university newspaper and they printed a photo of her. A local TV station picked her story, and she was on the *Wake-Up Charlton* show at the end of the program in the city curiosity section, interviewed by the weatherman. Isobel did not consider this flattering but was grateful for the publicity. It was something, and she was pleased as people began to seek her out or read the words she posted. It was gratifying if somebody from outside the academic circle inquired about her or her method, and she was most excited when she began receiving emails from authors, agents and publishers asking about her advertising rates. That is when she knew that she had become the billboard.

People were divided about Isobel and her t-shirt book. Some thought her noble, some thought her crazed, some wrote it off as a university stunt, but each year there would be an Isobel Emerson fan club who followed her blog religiously and made sure not to miss a day or an excerpt, still printed on the same white t-shirts, and collected the cards (and bought copies of her featured book). They thought she was a genius, which indeed she was. Some students began an Emerson topic on Reddit, and there was a lively digital discussion of her methods and the book she was promoting.

In her classes, Isobel encouraged her students to have a dialogue about her method, even if it meant omitting planned work from the current semester's curriculum. She was always open to suggestions on how to make her work go further. Her human billboard project grew in importance in her mind, and in the minds of those who read the t-shirts and took the cards. Isobel was on a quest for an organic, and maybe more primitive, method of disseminating information throughout society. She considered newspapers an antiquated device, which had fallen into the category of entertainment, and more dangerously, into propaganda based on who owned the press at any given moment. Instead, she championed the "book" in all of its forms. "A good idea, and maybe even a bad idea, is worth writing about," she would tell her class.

Over the years, her methodology—the t-shirts with their pocket of cards and daily quote did not vary—but sometimes she would play with the presentation. One year, on St. Patrick's Day, the t-shirts were green with white lettering. On Cinco de Mayo, she translated the day's quote into Spanish. At Christmas, she attached little silver bells to her shoes. On April 1, she slipped in a quote from another author and another book, to see if the students would notice and could guess who it was. On Chinese New Year, she misquoted her author to turn the day's text into fortune cookie prediction.

It took Isobel the better part of three years to complete her first experiment, by which time she had grown in popularity and achieved a cult status of sorts, even if her t-shirt method had not. Henry Sinclair and his publisher had given their permission to reproduce the book, thirty words a day (summer breaks, holidays and weekends aside) for six semesters. *The Instruction of Thomas Epperman* was now in its third printing; after the second printing, the publisher had sent her a cheque to help with the purchase and printing of her t-shirts (450 t-shirts, uniquely printed, did not come cheap). Toward the end of the third year, some of the earlier t-shirts were used in fundraising initiatives by her army of online and social media supporters, with a portion of the sales going to charity. A small amount was set aside to assist Isobel in the printing costs of her shirts.

The book's author, Henry Sinclair died that summer, and suddenly her project took on an added importance and recognition. Isobel had not expected long-term results, but she had hoped for them, and the startling success of her project laid the groundwork for more of her ideas to see the light of day. As an academic with a creative bent and her own ideas around communication, this was more than she could have wished for. Students flocked to her classes that were the most popular at the university, always filling up quickly with a waiting list. The renown of the 't-shirt lady" put the university on the map. People wanted to come and see the curiosity that was Isobel, five-foot-nothing, mousy gray cropped hair, baggy jeans, beat-up black Dayton boots and a t-shirt. Isobel never disappointed and she always ended her classes with the words of Henry Sinclair, "Go out and do something big." She wore *The Instruction of Thomas Epperman* every day, until she, and her t-shirts, were both old and threadbare.

Professor Angel

A nd that's why we feel that what you are about to learn here will equip you with everything you need: a cohort of supportive friends and future collogues, a questioning mind and . . . " the professor's voice in her ear trailed off as Alice's mind shut down.

"Positively pedantic," she said aloud to herself, (pedantic was her new word-of-the-day from her computer screen saver, she tried to use them often as she could after she understood what they meant), and she smiled as she bundled up her knitting and shuffled out of her seat. A few claps followed her out of the lecture hall.

Alice's job description was vague, which meant it was wide open to her own interpretation. She'd been hired because the university had "extra" money they had to use or they would lose the following year's gaming grant. So Alice had a job, and its description was . . . stretchy, or using a word from last week, it could grow in magnitude, in size or importance.

This week, for example, she was to go "shopping" with the first-years and listen to the introductory lectures by the professors. Shopping week was the first week of term where students could try different classes. She was the university's spy in the class. They were looking for information like the instructor's connection with the students, the freshness of the curriculum, class size and student

53

interest. So Alice would plop herself down in as many classes as she could for the first two weeks of term and prepare a report in her mind that she would write down later. She would usually pull out her bag of knitting, her water bottle and a few snacks and arrange them on the seat beside her. Rarely was a class so full that she could not use her adjoining seat.

A few of the professors recognized her and nodded in her direction when she was spotted, but most did not, being too absorbed in their first days of the new semester. The ones who did notice her didn't mind, because they were highly confident and actually enjoyed being tested like this. Alice loved these classes, the (usually youthful) professors had a bounce in their step and always looked freshly washed and pressed. She wasn't there to judge the teachers themselves, though she did; she was there to judge content, delivery and the "spark." She called it the spark because her ears would prick up when the room fell so silent that you could hear each student straining to listen to every single word. You could hear their breathing slow and their pupils dilate as they became enthralled; those two- or three-hour classes would feel only moments long.

It was nice for Alice to be in this environment again after the summer break, and she could feel herself absorbing the energy and youthful enthusiasm. She thrived on it. Her jobs with the University were varied, even though it was only for two semesters out of the year, but this was her favorite one, the fall semester, when everything was new.

Another of her roles, a lesser task, but still dealing with other people's fears, was to help the newly appointed head-of-house in each dorm to get set up with schedules and supplies: paper, folders, pens, eraser boards, microwaves, desks and a few kitchen things, and she would help each one out until they were flying on their own. Alice stayed around until they had successfully run their first student mixer and she could see by the level of noise and smiles that she was no longer needed. Then, like Mary Poppins, she would slowly and quietly remove herself and move on to the next scene.

Alice was also responsible for finding recipients for the various pieces of furniture and older tech set-ups that needed to be disposed of. She filled a gap here, because before she came, the old furnishings ended up in the landfill, wasted. Purchasing up-to-date furniture and supplies was another way for the university to use some of the money they received from the gaming fund grants, so Alice went around taking stock of what could and should be replaced in the various university offices, halls, labs, dorms and storage areas. Old chairs, tables, old but working microwaves, electric kettles and the like, would make their way to new homes, some on campus and some off, thanks to her ever-growing network. Various charities around town knew her and looked forward to her annual visits. She was like Santa, bringing furniture and equipment that was usually doled out to women's shelters, day-care centers, non-profit start-ups and most importantly to new immigrants who were starting all over in a new place, with nothing at all. Alice felt a bit like Robin Hood in this position and it suited her. She filled the gaps. She built bridges. The people she helped, some she saw and some invisible, went from having nothing to having something, after she used her magic and waved her iPencil in their direction.

The city next to the university campus had many cheap apartment blocks, with low rents, and, although it used to be a prized area, much of it was now derelict. In recent years, it had become the dumping ground for refugees when they arrived in this country, fresh off the plane. All of the tall apartment buildings huddled around a small city center which consisted of a church, a large grocery store, an elementary and a high school, a swimming pool, a hospital and a social service office. Apparently, somebody deemed that this was all one needed to begin a new life. Alice could relate and remembered what it was like for her when she got her first apartment, her first time living on her own away from home, the fear of it. This gave her empathy and compassion for this particular part of the job and she embraced it with vigor. There were always arguments amongst the higher-ups about who should to this job or that for people without a voice, and sometimes when they got caught up in arguing, they would forget why they were arguing in the first place and who they were arguing for, and that's how things got missed. This was how chains of communication and important tasks got broken and how people fell through the cracks, and Alice knew this was where she could come in and take over. She was of the perfect size to fit into these places and make bridges where none existed before.

The resettlement charity that assisted these newcomers was one Alice's beneficiaries, and sometimes in the fall, when she was rehoming unwanted items from the university, she would be called into a social service office to meet a newly arrived family. Other times she would meet them in their new home, which was usually an empty, small box apartment high up in the sky, the walls of which made her words of welcome echo. The people inside generally had nothing, and Alice knew what nothing was. Sometimes it was just a man, a wife and kids, and that's all. Not even a bag of clothes or a book. Sometimes they would already have a mattress or two on the floor, and some bedding, especially if winter was approaching, but that was usually all the charity could get ready for them. Often their arrival was not anticipated; they stepped off the plane and immigration had to take over.

Sometimes there was a newly installed, old-fashioned phone sitting on the floor, with an information package laid out beside it—usually a blue folder, sometimes in their own language but most times in English—telling them how to call 911, and listing some other numbers, including their new social worker's name and number. Alice would try to explain how to use the phone if they didn't know, act it out for them, showing them what buttons to push. Sometimes the people smiled or laughed, but mostly they just looked forlorn and tired. Sometimes they did not even know what to do with the strange food they had been given. If she had time, she would try to explain the packages or show them what was inside, or how to cook something on the stove, and if she had even more time, she would ride the elevator up and down a few times with the kids, letting them press all the buttons they wanted.

Although Alice was told where the people had come from and parts of their story, she preferred to hear and see it for herself. This afternoon's family included a pregnant twelve-year-old, the family having fled the country where the baby's father, the girl's militant older brother, still lived. Alice kept smiling, disguising her shock; all she could think to do was to show kindness, the same kindness that she had been shown when she was given this job, gentle understanding to these newcomers who were scared and hungry. The weight of this sadness was a lot for Alice to bear on her small frame, but she did her job as joyfully as she could. She smiled and touched their arms as she put down the bag with water bottles and a few snacks she had brought them, peace offerings. The language barrier was broken with these small gestures. She looked into the eyes of the family and tried to read their needs. It was not hard; a place to belong and a new start.

Next she went through each room, the whole family following

behind, making notes on her iPad in two columns; on one side
the document said, RIGHT NOW! and the other column was titled
LATER. Her notes were mostly one-liners or sometimes just a few
words—crib, bed, dresser, table and chairs, microwave, blinds,
the basics she knew she would be able to get her hands on. She
tried hard to focus on her work and not on their eyes, which were
hungry and hollow.

The next morning, back at the university, Alice walked through
the offices and residence blocks with a manager, making more
notes on her iPad. Mysteriously, within a few days, the pregnant
twelve-year-old would have a proper bed and a compassionate
doctor, and her mother and father would have a sofa to sit on and
a kitchen table with enough chairs for everybody. Now that Alice
knew the look of the family, the number and sizes of the children,
she would make a special trip to the Salvation Army store and buy
a few items herself, things that she couldn't find on campus. The
family would never know these gifts were from her, the small, smiling woman who had visited them in their new apartment. Alice
didn't expect to ever see them again, but she could feel their thanks,
and was happy she'd done her small part to welcome them to their
new home. One of the social workers called her a "goodwill ambas-
sador," and Alice liked to think that was part of her job, welcoming
people and showing them around. Showing up in the small quiet
spaces of a loud and busy world, she told herself, was one of the
most important jobs there was. She was in a place of power and
able to make great changes in people's lives. And for her, she could
think of nothing better.

The staff of the university called her Professor Angel, and she
loved this, because her own name, Alice, began with an A, and
she had quite a large collection of coffee mugs displaying the letter

A that she had been gifted by students and staff. The university boasted that they had hired Alice because she had "special needs," but then later on that label didn't matter anymore. She was Alice with the stretchy job: Santa, Robin Hood, Mary Poppins. Angel.

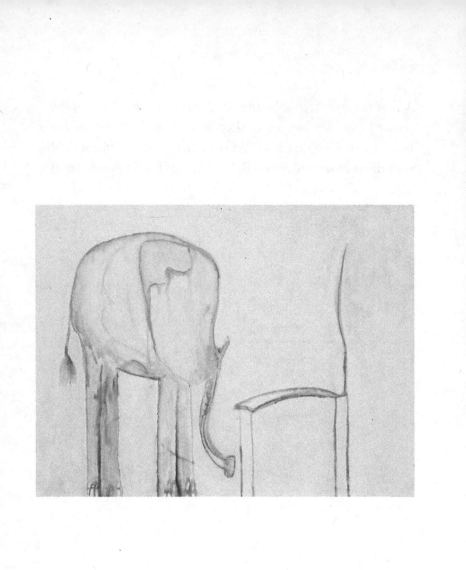

Still

A few times a year I start to feel the walls closing in. The house seems smaller and I realize that it's probably getting too cluttered in here. Although I watched Marie Kondo's program on decluttering religiously and even bought the book, the habits did not completely form and after a year of collecting old clothes and odds and ends and donating them to Goodwill each month, I'm afraid I fell off the "tidy" wagon.

Our house isn't exactly messy though. Rather it just begins to feel close when stuff starts to pile up—books, dog toys and even plants, especially because lately I've been on a succulent binge and my entire desk has been taken over by all the lovely shapes and colors. But, with three small, very active dogs and my husband Charlie in the house, it can feel a bit like a whirlwind of activity in here. Sometimes I know that it's also my mind that needs to calm and declutter too, and tidying the house will help with that, so last Saturday I flicked on the TV to watch Marie's happy little frame and rewatched my favorite episode, the one with the vet, and then felt refreshed and ready to revisit my clutter.

My purge lasted until exactly noon on Sunday and then came to a full stop when I came across the plastic bin of our old photos stored under the bed. I never know what to do with photos now, scan them and have them printed into a book? We have so many that they would fill countless albums. I guess our parents had the same problems when slides came out and everybody had a slide projector. Of course, they didn't do anything with them, we had a slide night exactly twice in my life when I was small, and then, the same as Charlie's folks, the slides and the old, (usually) broken projectors were handed down to us (where incidentally, they sit side by side in the back closet because we don't know what to do with them either). We've tried to look at the slides themselves, without the projectors, on bright days, but the ensuing headaches aren't worth it.

So on Sunday we sat going through photos. I lasted a bit longer than Charlie because he hates doing tedious stuff like this, not that he doesn't like helping, but because it's hard for him to stay doing anything for too long—it's hard on his body. Which is fine, I don't really mind because I was able to linger over our wedding album and recall the day and the days afterward and then I found my favorite photo of all.

The thing I love about this picture of Charlie is how still and serene he is, with his flash of smiling eyes and his mouth open just enough to make his dimples even deeper. We were on our honeymoon in Bali and ran out of film, and a nice Greek couple lent us their camera for a few photos. I took this shot of Charlie beside an elephant, but we laugh because I didn't even manage to get all the elephant in the shot. We offered to pay for the film, but kind couple shook their heads no, and when they found out we had just been married the gentleman unclipped a keychain off his backpack, a metal one with the Greek flag on it and handed it to us with a smile. (We love when strangers come together in travel;

it's like we're all instant friends and it gives us hope for humanity.) Those people were so kind, and that day was so amazing, and I loved Charlie so much already back then, I never knew time would increase that by leaps and bounds year after year.

Although the Polaroid is small, it is made big in my hands because of my huge respect for my husband. And I love it because he is so still, whereas in reality, sometimes looking at the live Charlie in front of me hurts my eyes and makes a small earthquake in my brain. In fact, sometimes I have to look away when we're talking, and I know how painful that is for me to do, so I can imagine how painful it is for Charlie, to see me doing it.

He wasn't always like this; decades ago when we first met, he had just the odd movement he couldn't control. His toes curling in, his leg twisting for no reason and, oh, he would get writer's cramp, really badly, so he couldn't open his hand after scribbling a few words with a pencil.

Sometimes if he was stressed or tired, or maybe too hot, his neck would get a bit jumpy and his head looked like it was shaking. These days it happens almost all the time, except when he is lying down, and he lies down a lot, so we can talk and so he can just have a break. His muscles get sore and tired from firing and fighting against each other all the time. I can't imagine his pain and frustration. Sometimes his head actually gets stuck looking to the left and he jokes that he's "leaning a little left" on those days. Sometimes the Botox treatments work to relax his muscles, but sometimes not. We've tried the DBS (Deep Brain Stimulation) with some result, but nothing lasts too long. But we're hopeful, the more of his special exercises he does, the better he is, we know he's rewiring his brain, so we keep up a pretty good regime, and dystonia isn't life threatening so we're happy and grateful.

And Charlie's a gentleman, does everything he can manage, and when he's lying down, he's just my old Charlie, cracking jokes and talking about life. We talk a lot about life, his viewpoint is so unique, and when we talk, I see the world differently. He's my hero. His continuous movement has pushed him beyond his body, and instead of being sullen or angry, it is like he has transcended. He talks about ideas and philosophizes and creates solutions for bigger problems. He has moved outside of himself.

At night I put splints on his legs and his wrists so his body doesn't get pulled out of shape while he sleeps. For some people like Charlie, the muscles contracting can pull the joints out of alignment, and since we would like to avoid surgery if we can, we splint and we yoga. Charlie is an amazing Yogi. Even though he can't physically do a lot of the positions, he tells me that his yoga is a mindful state, not a physical state, and I can feel the calmness around him. That's why sometimes it's hard to see him in such rapid movement, tremoring and spasming, sharp sudden jarring movements or slow repetitive ones. It's against his nature.

At first, doctors diagnosed him with multiple sclerosis, but after many clinic visits, tests and long lines of doctors, we just stopped and stood and then finally stepped outside the whirlwind of the medical system. We were done, and then by fluke, after Charlie had fallen down a couple of times, tripping over his own foot, we were sent to a new neurologist. We had already given up at this point and were serenely living our best life, Charlie's best life, and we were content. Well, as content as you can be with your neck stuck in one direction and the rest of your body in spasm. Our new doctor undiagnosed MS and gave him a new diagnosis of dystonia. She also gave us all kinds of hope and now we look forward to a day when his body might be tranquil, and move under his own direction, instead of Charlie having to work around his brain's odd decisions.

I show him the old Polaroid picture when he's lying down and he can see it clearly then too, because his head is propped up on pillows and he's not moving as much, and we both love it for the same reason: the look on his face is happy and restful and there is an elephant, but we don't always see it, and in the photo, Charlie is still.

Pee

Allison sat on the edge of her bed and tried to pick up the tea towel with her toes. Right foot, left foot, then she scrunched it up into a ball with one foot and then the other. It was exhausting.

By the time Amy, her always cheerful care worker arrived, often with a couple of coffees she'd grabbed from Moe's on the corner, Allison had usually completed her morning exercises and was happy for the help with breakfast and washing.

Allison's stroke had been a complicated one which had left her not only with paralysis but several other deficits, including anosognosia, which the doctors told her was "denial." For the first month after her stroke, she could not recognize the left side of her body. It took a long time to understand that her left side belonged to her, and was not, in fact, somebody lying in the bed beside her.

When she first woke up in the hospital's ICU, she had no idea why she was there, and when they told her she had suffered a stroke, at the age of forty-three, she was incredulous. She fought the idea like she fought the alcohol withdrawal that she was suffering from as well. She was pure, hot denial in those days, mostly of the idea that her drinking had led to her stroke. So it seemed natural that she should also deny half of her own body. Allison's reckoning had been slow in coming, but the stubbornness and resolve that had helped her through a month in the rehab facility was also helping her get through the days and hours of her recovery at home. Which wasn't easy. Exercises or daily challenges aside, she had too much time to think back on her life and look at the dark bits within her quiet bedroom walls.

The leisurely reviewing her life before the stroke shamed her for the most part. Megan, her counselor, came to her weekly to help her work through her past and her feelings as much as she could. She also introduced Allison to the twelve-step program and hooked her up with Meredith, who became her Alcoholics Anonymous sponsor. Allison was in touch by phone or email with Meredith daily, sometimes more than once, to help understand her cravings. Between Meredith and Megan (and other things that started with M, like meringue pie) Allison was slowly peeling back the blanket that had been cast over her life so many years ago. It was difficult to face the lies and untruths and small deceptions, but with so many hours in the days now, hours of sitting with nothing much else to do and fatigued from her rehab, Allison focused hard on each memory as it returned to her, and tried to think of it as a gift. Like the stroke. If it were not for the stroke, she was afraid to think of where she would be and who she would be hurting.

Allison also had motor apraxia on her stronger side, which they discovered once she began to recognize her body again. This meant that she had to relearn things like picking up a cup and brushing her teeth. Her brain felt disconnected and that was the scariest part of all. She had to remind herself of her progress daily, small as it was.

After the stroke, Allison had so many questions: simple things like how would she get dressed or feed herself or would she need to wear diapers; and bigger things like could she have sex, how long until she was "better" and if she could ever look forward to driving or being independent again. She also wondered a lot about how she would manage on her own, especially for things like cooking and bathing and household tasks like laundry. There was nothing she was going to be able to do without help, and more than once she broke down and sobbed over what she called The State of Allison. It was a very different place to the one she had been living in for the past decades, a place her mind never once had visited, while she smugly thought herself different from the friends and family who came to terms with their alcoholism or other addictions. She never once put herself in their company, even though they were all part of the whole, part of the fabric of her life.

Before her counseling began, Allison would panic when she wondered how she would buy her favourite wine, how she would cope without it. Instead of letting the panic grow, she would contact Meredith who would talk her down. As she became able, she made notes in her journal, the things she wanted to talk over with Megan, the things she could plan for and the new systems she could put into place and into practice. Allison started running her life, rehabilitation and recovery like a well-organized business venture, and she was finally starting to feel that she was succeeding in her newly modified existence. Her progress was now faster than the speed of her worrying thoughts. "Old habits," she would repeat to herself like a mantra, "those were old habits for an old life."

Half an hour after Amy arrived, Allison was up, had been helped to shower, had had her hair washed, was dressed and sitting in her wheelchair beside the window with a plate of fruit and a coffee beside her. She and Amy, who was going to be on holiday for the next two weeks, were going over the week's schedule. Steadman's, the nursing agency, was pretty good, and Amy was giving her a bit of intel about the new staff who would be coming to her. There would be a lot of new faces, but having been in management for years, Allison felt confident that she could still work with people.

After Amy left, Allison began writing in her journal, in big sloppy slow handwriting about the improvement of each body part and what she felt she had to work on. The previous day's entry read: *R foot ok, L foot too slow, breathing exercise, ok today but forgot to look at my left side while I was trying to move it. Forgot who it belonged to again.* And then a big smiley face with a lopsided grin.

At the back of the journal was a section marked "Private," like the "Keep Out" sign on a child's fort, where she wrote things about herself she did not like to revisit, but which she made herself share with Megan: *Why did I lie about being tired and needing a day off? I didn't need to lie, so why did I?* or *How old was I when I lost my self-esteem, did I ever have any?* These were thoughts that passed through her mind like clouds, and where once they would have sent her right to the bottle, now she just watched them form and float by. While she still felt the pain of them, when she closed the journal every entry had helped her brain inch forward a bit more.

The journal was partly for her and Megan and partly for her physical therapist, Aarif. He had been a physician in India before coming to Canada and became a PT rather than trying to requalify. Allison felt very fortunate in having his expertise on the matters of her health and recovery, and tried to be as detailed as she could. Aarif was also very good at deciphering her writing, which in these early days meant a lot of word substitution, as her hand did not always write what her mind was thinking.

Halfway through the first week of Amy's vacation, Allison was fatigued by the onslaught of new faces and the "managing" she had to do with the less experienced carers. One was painfully embarrassed about the personal care tasks—helping her into the shower chair or onto the toilet—and made silly mistakes. Allison had to direct them how and when and in what order to do things. She put on her bravest face and made jokes but it was exhausting and Allison was usually thankful to hear the door close behind them.

On the following Friday, a week after Amy had left, Allison sat slumped a bit sideways on the edge of her bed, slowly and conscientiously completing her exercises: right foot towel scrunch, left foot same, box breathing practice for a few minutes: inhale, count four, hold for four, exhale, count four, hold for four. Then a few short meditations from her iPad playlist and some sensory stimulation where she would try to feel each body part and finally a few minutes of stretching as best she could. It was exhausting and her stomach rumbled by the end of it, which took about half an hour.

She glanced at the clock on her bedside table and saw that the worker was fifteen minutes late. She always gave them a half hour's grace, because she knew the buses could be late and the city was expecting a wildcat strike any time now.

If . . . if the bus drivers had walked out, if there was a snowstorm, if there was a flu, if she had another stroke. She shook her head—she wouldn't let her mind go to that worrying pit of what-if panic. Some days it took all her strength not to go there.

She glanced at the clock again. Half an hour had gone by and Allison could feel the pressure in her bladder. She looked over at the phone beside her bed—had she somehow missed a call while deep in her exercise concentration? No, the message light was not flashing. She didn't want to be one of those people who called the agency all the time, one of the "burdens." She could do it on her own, make it to the bathroom. A month ago, when she could move the tea towel with her toes, that had made her so proud. She was getting the movement back on her paralyzed left side, although her eyelid and mouth still drooped, so sliding herself into the bathroom, only a few yards away, should be no problem.

She tried to sort out methodically how she could get there, just as she used to rehearse a meeting in her mind, sometimes days in advance. Or like how she would script a conversation, so there would be no mistakes, and she would look poised, no matter how drunk or how hungover. Allison could fake anything with enough rehearsal. This cloud flitted through her mind, but she saw it and let it go—there were more urgent things to work on right now and so she prioritized. Her plan, now that she had decided to do it, involved a number of steps, a number of small perfect movements, that would see her come off the bed gracefully and make her way to the bathroom without much effort at all. This was the way her brain was used to working. Nobody would know, nobody would see, it would all be easy with no consequences.

Her electric wheelchair was past the end of her bed close to the window and a walker, not yet used, stood in the corner waiting for her, for when her right arm and leg could be trusted. Allison's plan: slide off the bed, get to the wheelchair, pull herself into it and get to the bathroom. It would be easy to get from chair to toilet. The bathroom was fifteen feet away from where she sat, and the urgency of her need was pushing her on.

She took a breath, gripped the blanket with both hands and shuffled her bottom to the edge of the bed. She leaned back and put all her weight on her right leg. Then, very slowly, she slid herself off the edge of the bed, using her better leg to keep her body pinned to the side of the bed while she tried to control the slide down the side of the mattress. It worked, until she reached the point where the box spring ended, about thirteen inches above the floor. She hoped her leg had the strength to support so the bump wouldn't be too bad. She let herself drop. The jolt banged at her tailbone. "Thank goodness for junk in the trunk," she whispered out loud, laughing at herself.

The thigh and calf of her right leg were trembling from the exertion. That was the most strenuous work she had done since the stroke ten weeks earlier. Although her muscles felt strained, her bladder felt more stressed and so she shuffled on her bottom toward the end of the bed. Never had she loved the look of her wheelchair more, but she was feeling that there may not be time to get to it. She decided in that moment to bypass it and head right into the bathroom. If she was going to have an accident, she wanted it to be on tiles and not the expensive wall-to-wall wool carpet that covered her bedroom floor.

The dead weight of her left side was like a big sack of laundry that she had to drag along. As Allison sometimes still did not recognize her limbs as her own, instead of just pushing them out of the way she began to order them around: *Come on arm, you know you're mine, let's get this done!* She imagined herself a drill sergeant on one of the old military shows she loved, *Come on, leg, let's get a move on!* But this was even more tiring and she was getting a pain in her neck from the strain of having to twist her head to check on her progress. The stroke had also left her mostly blind in her left eye and she had to crane her neck around to make sure her left side was there, even while she bellowed instructions to it. Part of her mind kept thinking how funny it all was. *The failed contortionist.* But she couldn't laugh because losing bladder control

73

was becoming a real threat, not to mention her bowels ,which were now in on the game too, having gotten excited by all the activity and her straining abdominal muscles.

From her side she flipped and fell forward onto her stomach and wriggled and pushed and pulled herself another few inches. With her right leg she gave one final push off the bedpost at the foot of the bed, which scooted her six inches closer to the bathroom.

Her skin burned from rubbing against the rug, and her right side body felt bruised and raw, but she was getting there. She tried not to feel angry that the care worker had not shown up: something must have happened, so how could she blame her? Or was it supposed to be a him today? Nobody else was to blame here. She was here on the floor in this predicament, and it was nobody's fault but her own either. The stroke had been random, no signs or symptoms, just a spontaneous fluke the doctors had said, but also a direct result of years of two bottles of wine a day, mixed with a heavy concoction of Tylenol and aspirin for hangovers. *My body hadn't stood a chance.* She paused to take a controlled breath, to let this thought and blame pass like a cloud. She focused on moving ahead, inch by inch.

Allison stopped to rest and looked back at the bed while she tried not to look back at anything else in this past year, and it gave her some comfort seeing how far she had come from the rumpled sheets and Franklin the teddy bear. Her mom had sent her the stuffed toy and a potted ivy plant for her bedside when she had come home from the hospital. Franklin was watching her from the floor, having been toppled onto the carpet when Alison had slid out of bed. She laughed when she saw him lying there. With one half of her face she smiled at him, but as if her other side knew a secret, it did not smile, and instead something else tugged at her when she thought of her mother and the gift, and a darker cloud passed by. Her heart raced and she felt raw inside and out.

It was not uncommon for curious or painful memories from her childhood and past to come forward and present themselves to her now that she was going through her twelve steps, but there was always one memory that was just a little out of reach, it was buried and covered up with all the detritus her mind could pile on top of it. *Of course it would come today, no, here while I am stuck and looking like this.* Allison looked down and her t-shirt was stretched so that her right shoulder was coming out of the neck hole and half her right breast was popping out to say hi as well, it was as if she was being birthed out of the top of the Rolling Stones concert souvenir. For a moment she felt the floor shaking like in an earthquake, but then she realized that it was her whole body was shaking, even the bits that she couldn't feel and she was all at once elated and terrified of what would happen next. The memory came over her like a wave—it wasn't painful exactly, but she could almost feel her brain pull away and huddle itself into a safe ball.

A bit of pee escaped into the cotton gusset of her underwear. Urgently, Alison began to move again. Push, drag, pull, reposition, over and over again, until she reached the bathroom and could pull herself across the door jamb with her aching arm muscles.

Once she was completely inside, she lay on her side and rested her cheek on the cold of the bathroom tiles. She smiled to see how clean the floor was. Her apartment had never shone like this before the stroke. Thank you, Amy.

Alison's stomach grumbled. It was well passed her breakfast time now too, and her lower abdomen felt distended; she was getting scarily close to a big mess. At least she was just wearing underwear and her t-shirt and wouldn't have to worry about removing pajama bottoms.

Inching her way across the cold tile, she berated herself for buying the apartment with the larger bathroom, but in the same thought was thankful that it was attached to her bedroom.

Another few inches. Her face was red, her hair stringy and her body slick from sweat; her shoulder pounded hotly from the exertion of her fifteen-foot trek. Every muscle she could feel was cramping from the strain, and her brain felt like it had been run over by a train, as the sights and smells of childhood came back to her and kept her company on the last of her journey.

She had just reached the base of the toilet when the phone rang. The answer machine cut in after three rings and she could hear the beep that meant a message had been left. No matter: she was more concerned by the frantic urgency of her bladder and bowels, not sure which she feared more. At the foot of the toilet, she stopped to figure out how to pull herself up onto the seat.

Using the last bit of strength she had in her abdominals, she half pulled, half flopped herself up to a seated position and pulled her left arm into her lap. It was much easier to deal with when she could see it. *Hello arm, what's going on with leg?* Her left leg was at an odd angle, and she bent over, grabbed the top of her sock and tried to pull it into a more natural position.

Now that she was no longer lying on top of it, the pressure in her bladder was relieved a bit. As she gripped the shining white, cold toilet seat, Allison was again thankful it was so clean. She remembered to some toilets she had seen: flashes of club bathrooms, stall sex with strangers and waking up on bathroom floors covered in vomit. She had felt strong and secure at the helm of her life, getting herself from employee to upper management in a blink. Now slumped on her nice tiles, she could see she had just been building walls around her broken heart. Walls of bottles and bathrooms. Pee started leaking again.

She bent her right knee and shimmied herself up, pulling in her now bent left leg, trying to balance, and it sort of worked. Her bruised kneecap screamed and she knew her right leg was reaching the limits of its usefulness.

She tried next to pull her left toes up, just like when doing her towel exercises, as she would need them to help push as she pulled her left side's dead weight up onto the seat. Then she realized that the lid to the toilet was down. She pushed it hard so it clattered against the porcelain tank and held her breath when it looked like it might slam back down on her fingers. But it stayed put and she let her breath out a little but kept going. She was well past urgent now.

Her left hand slipped as she tried to heave herself up, and Allison was sweating so much she could feel moisture dripping off the tip of her nose. The bathroom was dark, and it was a gray fall morning, so not much light came through the rippled glass in the window. She wiped her hand on her t-shirt and tried again.

"Mental note to self," she said out loud. "Tell Aarif to prepare patients for this eventuality." She wished she had taken up her sister's advice to get an Echo unit; she would have been able to call somebody for help, even from her position in the bathroom. Why had she not just picked up the phone and called somebody? Old habits die hard. Why had she thought she would just pee first and then sort out the rest?

She berated herself for a few moments and the anger gave her a bit more strength, and she was up and standing, one hand on the toilet tank as she balanced on her shaking right leg. Then slowly sliding her hand, she moved it up to the hand towel rack, and she grabbed onto a towel that was hanging there, hoping the rack could hold her weight and the turn of her body. Her left arm dangled down in front of her, almost touching the seat. "Hello again, left arm I see you," she said. Then with one final, shaky effort, she twisted herself around and down onto the seat. Sweat dripped off her chin and she could feel her t-shirt was soaked through as she leaned back gratefully against the cold tank.

Then she peed right through her underwear. She couldn't believe how much was coming out, and remembered the scene from *Dirty Rotten Scoundrels*. "I am doing better than Steve Martin ever could!" and she laughed over the noise of the urine splashing into the bowl, muffled as it poured through her cotton panties.

Hot relief. Ecstasy. So many good words to describe this, she thought.

Tears still smarted the corner of her eyes but her position was too precarious to let go of the toilet to wipe them away. Bladder dealt with, she resolved that her next step would be to get her underwear off, just in case she should need to go number two. But for now, she leaned on the cold back of the tank and sighed and rested, her pounding heart slowly returning to a normal beat and her mind rearranging itself into a less painful and sporadic matrix, the past and present beginning to fuse itself together.

She imagined Aarif creating a sort of household "Olympic Games for Stroke Survivors," which could include The Bathroom Crawl, Brush Your Teeth Balancing, the Putting on Your Socks Challenge and, everybody's favourite, Cement Your Life Together with Bathroom Tile Grout.

She laughed again and then heard the key jiggling in the lock of her front door.

Sundown

I just realized that I've been using Ann's peppermint foot butter as a deodorant. The packaging is identical, that's why. It probably still works though. Let's try. I'm not sure why she's hiding it in her underwear drawer; when she does that I keep forgetting where it is.

The days are getting longer now, and though I am happy for the extra light, I can tell Ann is becoming concerned about my behavior now that it's unobscured by winter darkness. I feel a deep stress that, for me, shows itself in weeks of sleeplessness and, well, overeating. Sometimes I forget what I've eaten and I still feel hungry so I just eat more. I have to loosen my belt most days, I can't remember which hole to put the metal thing in.

I wondered about that yesterday and shuddered at the thought that I might be changing. Not just getting old, but changing in a way that scares me to think about; where like sometimes when I can't sleep, or I forget things I've just said or I repeat myself, and it's like I can't stop and sometimes Ann stares at me with her concerned look. The look where her face gets crinkly and I feel like I'm in trouble.

A few years ago, Ann and I finally reached that happy medium spot at the intersection of being finished with one part of our lives and the beginning of the next. It was a clear division for us, having both retired when we were fifty-five. It was freeing and pleasant.

But yesterday I turned fifty-eight.

Yesterday I wondered if turning fifty-eight was the age where you suddenly become old, obsessive and addled. Was I only ever looking at Ann as a parent now, searching for signs of her crinkled face and frown? Was she always staring at me? I looked at her face to see what she was thinking and tried not to let her catch me looking so I got back to looking at my book, but I couldn't figure out the lines, the words were jumbled and hurt my eyes. Was Ann angry? I went over every single thing I'd done in the day, every interaction we'd had, looking for the fault line. Then, like I usually do, I had a nap.

Sometimes when I feel very awake, which is more and more often in the middle of the night, I try to reach back in my mind to remember how I felt about Ann once, when I see her sleeping peacefully beside me. We were so in love and would do crazy things, travel on a whim, or do risky things to express our love, drinking Ayahuasca in the Amazon, or jumping out of a plane together holding hands. It scares me to think of those unsafe things we did. I don't like that unsafe feeling now, and sometimes I feel like it's Ann's fault. Like when sometimes she moves my chair and doesn't put it back and it makes me scared and something else, mad maybe. Angry.

The love is still here, I think, but it's topped off with a big swirly dollop of concern. Both hers and mine. I push it away with my spoon to see what's underneath and it's a blue bowl full of fears, bits of crunchy things. I don't know what they are anymore, and I don't want to look. Some liquidy stuff that looks messy and drops off my spoon onto my page, and finally, at the bottom, I find them—some solid blocks of the old love that have been broken into rocky chunks over time. They're mixed with a handful of daily pills that sometimes make me sleepy or agitated. I feel like the pills are making me worse and I blame Ann; she is the one who gets the prescriptions, she gives them to me and, when I say no, I sometimes find them hidden in my food or powdery at the bottom of my teacup. She thinks I don't notice.

Now I try to keep a checklist to keep things straight. Sometimes I write it down. I have a notepad with a black cover. I try to write down ideas, but it's hard to read what I write and sometimes I can't find the pen. I think maybe Ann hides my things. Sometimes I want her to write something for me, but I can't make the words come out. Sometimes I feel trapped in this body.

Is Ann acting odd? Yes. Check. But maybe it's me, maybe I'm agitated or getting paranoid. But sometimes I know it's her because she's incoherent and mumbles. I can see that cracks are showing through her polished armor. I try to scroll through the list in my head but it makes me very tired to think so much. Ann reads to me: "Sometimes dehydration can exacerbate confusion," and she asks me if I'm thirsty. I recall what we had for dinner last night; "Was the gravy too rich?" she asks me when I double over in a pain, "Were the potatoes too buttery?" I don't know if it's in my head or my stomach, I can't tell where it hurts anymore.

I scan the room: is it too hot or too cold? I check what I'm wearing: do I have my slippers on? She reads more from a little green pamphlet she has gotten from somewhere: "Temperature can affect moods," she's saying and scans me like a science fiction android—an imaginary green grid moves over the room and I know I'm fidgeting. I feel agitated even though I'm in my favorite chair, and I'm wearing my winter coat and a rainbow-striped toque which usually makes me feel good and comfortable and calm. Temperature does affect my mood. Ann is right. I smile at her when she's right and sometimes she gets tears in her eyes.

The checks on my list don't balance all the time, the scales tip.

I measure my findings and the graph is plotted—dementia. The doctor said it, and Ann told me one day and sometimes has to remind me. Sometimes I understand and I try to plan for the day when maybe I'll jump off the bridge or get some medication from my doctor and end it all so Ann won't have to deal with me. Right now we're leaning starboard. My brain fires away full throttle, checks and balances rule my days now, and my vocabulary is filled with adjectives and adverbs: calm, happy, grumpy, clumsy, agreeable, peacefully, slowly; sometimes I can't even think in full sentences. My thought processes have been reduced to a shopping list of omissions and flaws, Ann's facial expressions and my striped toque which I want with me more and more.

Nobody tells you how to get old, or old and sick. You don't get training wheels for this stuff. I try not to let anxiety overtake me, but some days it's difficult when you're not very brave, and I fear the future for me and for Ann. The fact is, I don't know if I can do it without her; she has been my center of gravity for so long, I forget what my own weight feels like and she is fading from me. I called her "mother" once and she cried. Some days I forget who she is all together and can't remember her name.

She tells me I'm brave. It's certainly not bravery that impels me forward, just stubborn strength that pedals me up the hills. But instead of riding beside me, Ann is behind me, like we're on a Schwinn tandem, and more and more she is doing all the pedaling.

I'm not brave. I just have to have arms strong enough to right us when dementia's gravitational force pulls us off balance.

Like last week, at the lawyer's office, where we'd gone to sign some important papers. The doctor had said that we should update our wills and living wills and other documents like a power-of-attorney before it was "too late." But it was already "too late." I couldn't remember why we were there. I didn't recognize the place and I got scared. I asked a question, and when I looked at Ann, looked into her eyes to try to understand the thought behind the garbled words that came out of my mouth, suddenly I knew. I recognized the glitch in my own thought process, and the blip on the radar screen that was telling me that I had probably passed my prime for signing any of these documents. I quickly looked up at the lawyer, his name was Walters, I remembered him now, from when we bought our house. He was old and past retirement age, much older than us but he was nearby and available and he always smiled. We liked him. He wore a sweater instead of a suit, a red bowtie instead of a tie, and he looked like a grandfather or tenured college professor. He reminded me of Mr. Rogers, like when we used to watch that show with our kids when they were small. I looked at him looking at Ann.

She'd made this appointment weeks ago, but even at the time when she was speaking to the receptionist, I felt a pang of guilt inside me when the secretary asked if I still had all my "faculties, and then I had felt downright criminal as Ann answered, "Yes." That was a big fat lie and I was angry at her again. I don't remember knocking the phone out of her hand, but I remember watching her cry and clean up her broken coffee mug.

I knew my mental capacity had declined rapidly since she'd made the initial appointment and if the grandfatherly gentleman in front of us deemed me incompetent in any way, it would cost half of our life savings to get Ann through probate once I was dead and gone. The stress of this made me feel agitated and dizzy and I kept forgetting what I was going to say so I tapped my hand on my leg, helping me to stay focused until Ann reached over and put her hand on mine to stop me. I almost got mad, but her hand was warm and it felt nice.

So I held my breath and tensed every muscle in my body, willing my mind to stay clear for just the next thirty minutes. Then I tried not to snap my head around when I looked at Ann. I forced myself to move in slow motion. I tried to hide my concern and soften my face. No sudden movements. But Ann saw, and her eyes widened when she realized I had wet myself. But I couldn't help it and I bit my tongue so I wouldn't cry and I could see her face start to crinkle up and I was scared.

I looked at the floor. She tried to save me and asked if I would hold her coat and she laid it over my lap. I grabbed it and it was warm and soft like a mother's blanket. She quickly changed the subject and said we needed to be going, if we were finished, and I was still sitting there holding the coat and garbling family members in my mind, stuck on the lawyer's words "next of kin." I couldn't figure out what it meant. I tried to ask and it didn't come out right, instead I said, "ambassadors are singing" and clicked my tongue afterward and then whistled, and I knew after it came out that it didn't make any sense. But Ann saved the day by hanging something shiny in front of the lawyer, a bigger question about his fees for this form or that form, asked quickly so he wouldn't see my confusion and wet pants or, if he had seen, wouldn't think too hard on it. Then Ann rallied and beamed at me, "Time to go!" and she rustled us out of that office so fast I didn't know what was going on.

We were saved: Walters, the lawyer, from having to address the confusion and consider my fitness and capacity to understand what I was signing; Ann, from embarrassment and from a truth that's rattling too fast towards us; and me, from having to commit to any diagnosis. If I didn't, maybe there could still be some flexibility. I'm afraid to stop trying, to fall into the black hole. I'm afraid.

Now I wonder where we are on this map. Now that the disease has come for us. Are we living a life of expectation, where every little thing pushes the compass needle in one direction? Is it too late now to take care of things the way I want them to be done? When I can silently slip away, steal out the door and to the bridge? Sometimes it makes me cry that I can't remember the way there anymore, and I know it might already be too late.

But when we got back home and were safe inside and I was in my favorite chair watching my favorite show, *Barney Miller*, on repeat, because Barney's voice is calming to me. I looked at Ann and decided right then to try and laugh with her more, try to get back the old feeling. I thought about writing that on my notepad but Barney was there smiling and I forgot about it.

I'll take what I can while we have it. I'll dig around down there in my calm place, inside my blue bowl, and bring it up on my spoon to see if I can remember what our old life tasted like. I'll try to be ready for whatever comes next, when I can remember, that's my goal. But for now, I'll try to be nicer to Ann and not let worry lead me another way.

Weather permitting, and storms aside, I can hold off the tipping point a bit longer. That time when I will no longer be able to save myself, understand my own thoughts or be comfortable. That time when my mind slips down and I can no longer bring it back up, and Ann will look at me and my eyes will be empty and I'll be gone. When we will sit here together and she will be with me, and I will be somewhere else, alone.

But today I'm not ready to go there. Today I'll make the most of what we have left and I'll put some of the old effort into it again, I'll help her make some pies like she asked, and we'll fill the freezer for her, for when I'm gone.

People Like Frank

The new microwave has a reminder function on it. It's so you won't forget that there is something in it, which we used to do all the time with the old one. You'd open it in the morning to find yesterday's cup of coffee, a cold half-baked spud or the like. Frank calls it the "senile setting" and the beeping drives him crazy. And it makes him angry that he needs it.

He'll start off a project, like replacing the bathroom fan, and then he ends up over across the other side of the house cleaning the rust off the porch light, every counter and table in between full of tools and bits. And then he gets mad that he forgot what he was doing and stomps back in to finish installing the fan. In the meantime, he's forgotten that he was warming up his second cup of coffee. Now the new microwave beeps at him, and he gets mad again. I'm getting used to him getting distracted, but I still hate the mess.

In the old days, our apartment was tiny and I had to clean up after him if I wanted to make supper or have a place to fold the wash. Over the years, he got better about putting things away. Now when I come across a hammer or other tool left out in the rain or the rake leaning up against the fence, looking lonely and forgotten,

I know it's not on purpose; it's that Frank doesn't remember what he was doing with it. We usually come across these things in spring, when the snow melts. I've stopped blaming him.

I think he has a bit more pride or maybe it's shame, and he'll come back and start to tidy up until he gets mad again and starts throwing things when he can't fit them back where he got them from. He's like that, flashy temper. There are lots of reasons why people get angry sometimes, and I think he's made up of all the reasons. He just can't help himself—it's such a habit. I'm used to it and I don't much like it, but I put up with it. I can't change him.

It didn't use to be this way. Frank has always been the kindest person. If you needed help moving, you didn't even have to ask, he would offer up and just be there with his truck, a pizza and a six-pack of beer. Back in the day, I would find him underneath the neighbor's car changing the oil, driving somebody across town to an appointment, or professing to me in the quiet and dark dawn that he wanted to be a better man. He would do anything for anybody, even people he didn't know. If you ask any of our friends, they would say he is *über* thoughtful and helpful. People *like* Frank. He is a small man with a big heart. I used to call him my love extremist.

Back in those days, nobody ever saw a temper, and I don't think he was angry very often, and if he was, it was only in private. Like when he would read of an injustice in the news and stomp around for a while trying to help find a solution, then send off a fiery letter to the editor offering up some suggestions. It was a gentle kind of anger, I wouldn't even call it anger; it was just passion and I was never afraid of it.

That is the Frank I fell in love with. And even though I know something about genetics, and even though I knew his parents and could see the life he came from, especially when they both fell into dementia themselves, I never imagined it would happen to him. Perhaps I was just naive or didn't want to know. When you are first in love, the last thing you think of is the bad or tragic ending that could be yours. It's hard to see past your next date, lovemaking session or first child, let alone thirty or forty years down the road when the change that has maybe started to happen on and off finally gets itself together enough to turn the gentle, funny and talented man that you loved into a monster that you now can't stand. Your own balance slides back and forth between compassion and fear, and the blankets bunch up between you in the bed like a new third person whose name is Apathy, because I've stopped caring altogether. It's hard enough just keeping up with him most days, never mind feeling regret. I can't—there's just no time in my day.

Sometimes Hate is his second name, like this morning when it slapped me in the face.

The dog's shit smelled like a hundred dead rotting things, and the putrid after-scent woke me out of a dead sleep and I felt exhausted at the thought of having to clean it up. The dog woke up ill, Frank said, but wouldn't tell me why. He was afraid to—probably the dog ate something on the trail or on their final toilet walk of the night. Sometimes he gives them big chunks of cheese without me knowing because he's afraid to lose their love, especially when they curl up with me at night—I can feel they are tense around him. But for the mess, Frank just let me deal with it, instead of possibly making himself feel worse because he can't focus enough. He gets distracted, and I don't blame him, it's not him, it's the disease and that realization makes me have all the feelings.

It's hard being a parent to your spouse, having to remind them when to eat or shave or when to take their medications or vitamins, when to put on clean clothes or even take a shower. It's all hard because you never see it coming. Frank and I were so in love and had our routines down, there were no cracks in our mutual armor, "us against the world" for so many decades, thousands of miles or happy road trips, writing songs and reciting poetry over breakfast, such a solid and complete life that you don't see the cracks when they start to form. The little niggly things that at first you write off to allergies or a cold, or a sleepless night. A surprise fight that blows up out of nowhere like a spring storm or a pair of socks shoved in the cutlery drawer. Misplaced reading glasses that you find months later in the freezer. Then you start to wonder what's going on. If I would have known then what I know now . . . I'd seen both of his parents with Alzheimer's, why didn't I anticipate it? After years of watching parents and our friends come to long, sad endings with various dementias, why didn't I see? I berated myself for some time but I think the answer is that I didn't want to see it, my denial was so strong, and I was just tired, tired to think that old life was still following us around, but this time without an escape, because it was in our own house and our own bed and not some miles away in another town, somebody else's problem to deal with. I was just too tired to see it.

I should have taken it on as a study project, like everything else I do. I research everything from which kind of vacuum cleaner to buy to which vitamins are the best. I take every online course that I have time for, and I am always wanting to know more about everything. So why didn't I spend my time researching the probability that Frank would develop the same disease his parents had, or something like it, and that it might even come early, in his fifties, right when we were starting to plan our retirement. Things we wanted to do, and trips we wanted to take. India was at the top of this list and we poured over its history, sitting for hours in front of the computer, making plans and routes. Then we thought we'd buy a small apartment in Italy and maybe retire there for a while until grandchildren came along, and we had lots of discussions about that too as we waited for happy news from our son, Tom, who was newly married.

I didn't wake up one day, just knowing. It was all of the small things that sort of dawned on me, as the saying goes, trite but factual. All the little things that start to add up, the odd bits of life, the misplacing things, the forgetfulness, the anger, all the things that just start getting closer and closer together until they start to seep into your understanding as the new normal.

We have oddest arguments about the strangest topics, Frank getting so angry when he can't make me understand a point he is trying to make. Last week we argued about not mowing the dandelions in spring because the bees need them, but Frank kept saying the bears needed them, and then it was beetles (because he couldn't remember the word "bees") and then something about a Beatles song and flowers and it just got really weird and I stood there and the realization seeped slowly over me like a sunrise inching up my body. It's gradual like that, an uncovering of the truth, with the disease showing itself a bit at a time, just here and there until it is all revealed. But by then you already know, because you can compare an old normal with the new and you can see that they are no longer a match. In fact, the new normal is so far off the scale, you cannot even call it any sort of normal; it is not even close to Frank's old character. That's when it all comes stomping into your brain and it wakes you up, because you damn well know the symptoms and all the first signs, and you can't ignore them anymore because the resemblance to his parents now pokes you in the eye and you can't even try to be in denial. You can only sit sad and dazed and realize that what you're feeling is the beginnings of hate creeping in, a simmering anger when you realize what your life is going to be like for the next few years. And you try to reassure him when he jokes about it, and you try not to feel guilty because you are already so tired from living and looking after dogs with dodgy stomachs.

Anyway, I got up to look after the sickly dog whose shit stank like a thousand fresh hells and whose stomach was gurgling and I left the door open in case we needed to bolt outside. I could hear a bear next door eating apples from the neighbor's abandoned tree and I didn't even care. Bears don't scare me anymore, rather this life does. I can put up with a bit of nature, it seems like nothing compared to being a parent all over again: eat your veggies and tie your shoes, put your warm coat on and don't wander out of the yard.

It's hard to be in that place again, especially with somebody who can drive. I can handle most of it, but I just don't like when he gets mad and forgetful when he's driving. That's the worst. On the road. Frank likes to do the driving—he says I go too fast. He will never go above twenty. He's overly cautious and we usually drive around with a cacophony of car horns following us and once a few weeks ago we got a ticket for driving so slowly and in a bike lane. He grips the wheel so hard and a frustrated sort of anger overtakes him. I hate it. He told the cop he was like a "dried turd on the bottom of his shoe," and I thought that would be it, the cop would get angry, and in my mind I saw Frank resisting arrest and being taken away, very much like in the police dramas we used to love to watch, and that maybe if all that did happen, maybe I could have a night off. But the characteristically undramatic officer just laughed, shaking his head as he walked back to his car, and I slunk a bit lower in my seat, beaten again.

Sometimes I daydream about when I'll have to try to take his keys away. They don't tell you about stuff like that when you're young, nobody gets you ready for that. It's not part of a Home Economics class and it's not in the books: *Hiding the Car Keys from a 65-Year-Old Time Bomb 101.* That's the stuff we have to deal with when we're older, although I don't feel old enough yet. I wish they had a course for it at community college, not just for the doer, but for the person we have to do it to, so they would know that at some point, like it or not, somebody else is going to be making those decisions about when you'll stop driving, when you have to go to the doctor's office, and when you have to do just about everything, because it will all become a battle if there is no understanding.

I try to imagine how that day is going to go, when I tell him I'm doing all the driving from now on. Frank ran over a cat last week and a few months before he came back home with a big green dent in the back fender. He wouldn't say how it happened and I was afraid to ask.

Frank won't get his eyes checked either, and that makes the thought of him in charge of the car even scarier. I figure something really bad will happen like he'll run over one of our elderly neighbors or their grandkids. Should I wait until Frank's so far gone he doesn't notice before I hide the keys? The same way we hid his dad's back when the old man used to drive around in his van with homemade moonshine in a Listerine bottle hidden under his seat?

Frank and I don't drink, so that will never be a problem, not like with Stan. I held my breath every day hoping he didn't kill anybody. He never did, just himself, slowly, with the bottle.

There should be a book about getting old, about how to do things and what you'll have to look forward to. A how-to book the government sends you when you're sixty-five, along with your Old Age Pension applications, so you can plan for it. The chapters might include "How to not feel ashamed when you need to wear Depends," or "Ways to love your spouse, when they no longer recognize you." Required reading. *The Things You'll Need to Know* could be the title.

It would be a book for people like me, who have to deal with people like Frank.

Glass

W indows are for looking out of, not for looking into." She remembered her mother repeating that line to her as they walked the streets in the early evening, when she made a remark about seeing families sitting down for supper together. She was fascinated with windows even then, the little vignettes behind the framed glass: a woman rocking a baby, a man and woman laughing and dancing, a child playing with a dog, an argument. They were the stories of life, but they were private and raw and her mother forbade her looking from that moment on. "You live your own life and they will live theirs, it's not your place to be a spy," she hissed with a smack atop her head. But she would still glance up when her mother's back was turned. It was just too good a show not to bear witness.

She never used the silent movies she observed. She never spoke of what she saw behind the glass. She never wrote about them, not even in her private journals; she just let them soak into her and they came out in other ways: in a smile, in a frown, in a laugh, in the way she would eventually arrange the flowers in her garden.

In the middle of her living room floor, one knee in genuflection, her head bent low to the ground she cried into the phone that she

95

held to her ear. The helpline girl (who sounded very young) carefully reflected back to her everything she said, until after a time Lina yelled, "Is this all you're going to do? Repeat what I say?" and then she fell on her side and stuttered and felt even worse. "Can't you offer me any real help?" she sobbed. She hung up, flung the phone across the room so hard it cracked and broke open against the wall, leaving two batteries rolling across the kitchen floor and under the fridge.

The call had somehow made things even more desperate and she cried her tired heart out over the batteries. Then she lay on the dank, cheap beige carpet, and when she looked in the mirror later, she saw the red mark imprinted across one side of her face. The house was a grand one, but living in its basement, with only three small windows, allowed little brightness and no views. Of course she understood that the basement had to be strong enough to hold what was on top of it, and so the luxury of light was not something built into the concept.

Upstairs, Harriet, her charge, was slowly sliding into dementia.

She had come to this new country as a language student, leaving behind a trail of sadness. But after a few months, all she had learned was that the school was corrupt and only legitimate on paper; and when that paper folded and the regulators closed it down, she found herself in desperate need of a legitimizing job so she would not be sent back. Which could not happen at any cost. This was her fresh page start—no cruel husbands here—and she was determined to not repeat her own mistakes. She felt this new place was her one chance to repair, rehabilitate and then construct a life of her own making. Turning a new leaf seemed too gentle a way to say it when she was ready to rebuild from the ground up. The phoenix rising, she changed her name as well.

Necessity drove her into many jobs that did not last: customer service at a Sunglasses Hut in the mall (dismissed—English too poor); carpet cleaning company (dismissed—not strong enough to haul the equipment in and out of the van); nanny (dismissed after a day—knew nothing about babies). There were about five others, none of which lasted longer than a week.

Too ashamed to stay in a women's shelter or hostel, and fearful of the immigration authorities who could send her right back home, she slept in a city park, a small, quiet woman huddled with her rolling blue suitcase inside a toy wooden house in a children's playground. The fat logs felt comforting and she imagined the people who built the structure being loving individuals, laughing as they worked, anticipating the joy of the many children who would play there. She would rest her head on the log windowsill and look out over the playing field, the cold sand beneath her absorbing the warmth of her body until she slept.

The summer sun woke her early enough in those days to leave the park before the morning joggers and children on their way to school filled the playground. Although some days she would sit on a bench and try to catch some of that youthful spark, mostly she wheeled her suitcase to the McDonald's nearby, the familiar arches, where she would wash in the bathroom and prepare herself for a day of interviews. The view from the restaurant's grimy window to the street below, when she lifted her eyes from the classified ads, was warmer but not as pleasant as the playground view from the children's log house.

Multi-sided desperation had led to a string of no-experience-required jobs, the ones that nobody else wanted. Then she discovered caring. The personal ads posted by exhausted people seeking respite from their own family members, mostly aging adults with incipient dementia. Not severely affected enough for them to be

JENN ASHTON

in a facility, but enough that their odd behaviors put extreme stress on everyone in their household. On more than one occasion during an interview, the son or daughter or spouse questioning her would break down and cry out of pure exhaustion.

She was always hired on the spot, her sweet, calm face, framed by dark hair with thick bangs, and her slight stature exuded a peacefulness that was often mistaken for confidence, even in her own mind. In truth, it was her empathy and willingness, her need to help alleviate a burden, which had gotten her into trouble in her previous life.

Lina awoke at 4:00 a.m. knowing her charge was out of the house. Harriet was waiting outside for the small yellow handy-bus, the kind with the wheelchair lift in the back, shivering in her coat with the fake fur collar. This was happening more often and Lina gradually began to lose sleep as Harriet's confusion worsened. She found herself on a twenty-four--hour clock, with no respite.

Sometimes Harriet would be fine and they could hold a conversation, other times she would try to attack anybody within reach with a kitchen knife, calling them a witch. On one occasion, she heard the back gate click and found Harriet standing outside the neighbors' big window, waving half a day-old loaf, crying and shouting at the bewildered couple that they were starving her. She put her arm around Harriet's shaking shoulders and led her back home.

When Harriet was having a good day, she smiled and laughed, but it never lasted for long and in the next moment she would be pounding on the door, yelling to the heavens that her cat had died. Rushing upstairs she would find the orange tabby cat asleep on the tidy bed, beginning a healthy purr and ready to stretch when his back was stroked. Along with the dead cat, Harriet would also see rows of dead people sitting on her beige floral couch, or in various prone positions throughout the house. Harriet would step over them as Lina tried to do housework, and she would cry or whisper to them when she thought nobody was looking. The situation deteriorated for many years before Harriet was even diagnosed with dementia.

Crying on the phone to the helpline more than once, Lina felt that she had done her penance and deserved a way out. She had earned her Canadian citizenship, passed her tests and was now lingering on the far side of middle age, becoming tired. When Harriet's son Ted, the last of her family, had a stroke at sixty-three, he had established a trust to ensure his mother received the best of care throughout her lifetime. At first, Lina had been honored to be named the trustee. She knew she was privileged and cried joyful tears that she was considered part of the family after so many years of hard work. But the privilege eventually felt like a noose, trapping her when she would have preferred to walk away. She tried several times to have Harriet placed in a home, but the waiting list was long and the weight of obligation heavy. There was nobody else to help advocate for her charge, who after a time would just sit with a blank stare or cry inconsolably for hours.

One scorching August day, just when Lina was sure she could not go on, she found Harriet in the living room, surrounded by a fabric storm. The couch was shredded and there were banks of cut-up clothes and tea towels and bedding across the beige carpet. Seated in the eye was Harriet, on the now shredded couch cushions, a big pair of sewing scissors still in her hand. The elderly orange cat was cat purring on her cold lap. The doctor said it had been a massive stroke.

Slowly Lina rolled up the blinds to see what the autumn had to show her. It never did disappoint, and this day's production included a bold yellow, large leaf sycamore with its spiky balls still green and fresh, in front of a line of green firs and cedars all set off by the backdrop of pale pink sky. Every window boasted a spectacular view, but autumn was the showiest season and she could feel a bit of the cold coming through the glass.

One of the things she loved most about her house was the glass. When she first stepped in the door, she went around and counted: thirty-one windows, fourteen skylights and two wood-framed glass doors. The light was incandescent, even though she had to sometimes block the skylights from the sun with sticky reflective window coverings and many paper and wood blinds, lest she broil in the summer heat. With these few seasonal modifications, and a new small heat pump/air conditioning unit stuck tidily on the wall between kitchen and living room, her small single level wooden house was perfect.

She never felt anything but happy in this house. She compared it to her past—forbidden windows and apartments in her early life, the children's play cabin, the drab basement holding up a mad woman's house—when there was nobody to build a space for you and you could only use what you had, or what was already there, when you were wholly exposed and only allowed to fit into somebody else's world.

She pondered that thought and wondered if houses were built like people. If the designers used their own story, in the making: "He was a military man, and as an architect, his personality was reflected in his builds. Solid bases with many floors on top, all bound together with layers of wood and painted smooth."

She laughed at the thought as she dressed. In the mornings she did not open the bedroom blinds until she was clothed, she never wanted to feel exposed again, even though her bedroom faced only forest. She was afraid of any eyes on her in the morning, in that personal moment where she stood in front of the mirror and made up her face. Just a bit of color here and there, to brighten her complexion.

The person who built this, my home, knew about the properties of nature, she said to herself over her tea. Sitting on a stool at the counter she looked all around. They would have known about the properties of light and mood, they would have known the soul's need to witness the leaves and snowfall; they would have known about color, like how the snow makes everything a contrast with the world, and they would have known people.

To build a planetarium, one had to know the stars; to build a woman, sometimes you needed to borrow somebody else's walls to provide structure and safety until she grew and it was time for her to leave. And on and on she thought about people and the things they built and how we lived and evolved in those spaces, and how we were drawn to and found the spaces that suited us best, or how we learned to live our lives, maybe in some places that didn't suit us best. She could never forget the little basement suite with only three panes of glass, and how it reflected the truth of her life for all those years and the ones before, how living in these places had built the person that she had become, slight and compassionate, now with a thick graying bang framing her serene eyes.

Keeper

C laudia Sherman's Keeper," he wrote on the form in front of him. He understood that everybody who entered the facility needed to be properly accounted for. He finished the form to the bottom, filling in as much detail as he could before he signed his name, spun it around and handed it to the lady behind the desk.

The stout woman behind the desk received the form, held it up closer to the big ceiling lights and then put on her reading glasses to read the man's very tiny handwriting. She looked at him again and then back at the form.

"Have a seat please." She nodded to the peeling green vinyl-covered chairs in the corner of the long room. She watched him lumber to the chairs and plop himself down in one nearest the wall. He humphed under his breath but she didn't hear him.

He watched the second-hand ticking on the big white-faced clock opposite him, while the receptionist put his paper into a cream file folder and placed it in a black plastic tray on the corner of her desk. When the clock's hands met at the top, high noon, there was a buzzing on the receptionist's desk and he could hear her mumbling something into the phone receiver.

"Mr. Cheevers, the doctor will see you now. Please follow me." He lumbered up out of the chair and followed her through a door and into another small room with another chair and another door.

"Please wait here," she said, but before he could settle his bulk into the new chair, the other door opened and a small, bespectacled man appeared.

"Come this way," he said, in a voice that matched his stature. He pointed to yet another chair opposite an old green faded metal desk and then left briefly, coming back with the file in his hand.

"Mr. Cheevers, thank you for seeing us today," he said looking at the single page in the folder as he moved to the other side of the desk and sat down. "I hope you are feeling well?"

"Well enough," Mr. Cheevers answered, moving uncomfortably in the small chair. He needed to be just so, sort of sideways, to fit all of himself on the seat in between the two arms.

"Can you tell me the reason you think you are here today, Mr. Cheevers?" The doctor put down the file and picked up a pen. It was not just any regular pen, but a floaty one with a tiny sailboat. Mr. Cheevers watched the doctor tip the pen one way and the boat sailed into a sunset. The doctor flicked his wrist and the sailboat headed toward a dock. Mr. Cheevers watched the doctor slide the boat back and forth a few times before he cleared his throat and answered.

"Does it have something to do with the blue car?" he asked.

"It is not for me to tell you," the doctor said. "Rather it is for you to try to tell me why you are here." He abruptly put the pen down with a clack on the metal desk.

"Er, yes. The blue car then. I think it has something to do with the blue car." Having made up his mind, Mr. Cheever tried to sit up straighter by way of punctuation. "The blue car and the dog that was barking and . . ." Mr. Cheevers stuttered and stopped and looked at the doctor.

"Tell me about the dog."

"He was barking, barking loudly."

"Why was he barking so loudly, Mr. Cheevers?" the doctor asked, his voice solicitous.

"Because of the screams." Mr. Cheevers said, uncomfortable in the chair, which felt smaller by the minute. In fact, he thought, it was as if the chair was trying to hold him down, its armrests closing in and pinning his arms in place. He crossed his arms in front of his chest like a superhero and held them tightly in that position, up and away from the grabby armrests.

"Screams?" the doctor asked. "What screams might those be?"

"The screams of my mother."

"Ah, I see. Now we're getting somewhere." The doctor leaned towards Mr. Cheevers, noticing that the large man's arms were now shaking from the exertion of holding them in the odd position. "And why was your mother screaming?"

"She was screaming because of the prize."

"The prize?"

"Yes, she received a phone call in the car saying she had won a prize, and the dog went crazy, jumping up and down and my mother was screaming about the prize and the dog was barking louder and it was hurting my ears." Mr. Cheevers covered his ears with his hands to mimic what he had done on the day. "It was so loud I could hardly stand it, the screaming and barking and excitement."

"And then what happened?" The doctor tilted his head at Mr. Cheevers.

Mr. Cheevers wriggled his bulky form, still trying unsuccessfully to find a comfortable position, so he stood up. Standing in front of the doctor's desk, he felt a little more secure because of his height and size.

"And then everything just stopped," he said. "My mother stopped screaming and the dog stopped barking and then I could see the book sticking out of the torn upholstery on the passenger seat of the car. It was as if something wanted me to see it there, so I walked over, opened the door and pulled the book out of the seat."

"What was the book, Mr. Cheevers? Can you describe it to me?" The doctor was making notes now on a yellow legal pad as the sailboat floated above the sunset.

"It was a sort of journal. It was red and looked pretty old."

"And what was written in it?"

"That's the thing. I don't know. I started to open the book and my mother grabbed it out of my hands and threw it to the dog who ate it." At this, the doctor dropped his pen, removed his glasses and looked sharply at Mr. Cheevers.

"The dog ate it?" The doctor repeated slowly, looking directly into Mr. Cheevers' eyes, in fact so directly that Mr. Cheevers got the uncomfortable feeling that the doctor's eyes might shoot lightning and fry his brain like an egg, so he shut his eyes and held them as tightly closed as he was holding his arms.

"Yes, sir. The dog ate it. It was a fair-sized book, a bit bigger than a regular paperback, but Harold is also a big dog, and, well, he just, ate it whole, or more like swallowed it, in a gulp." Mr. Cheevers could see the look on the doctor's face as he opened his eyes ever so slightly to peek. The Dr.'s eyebrows moved closer, looking like two furry brown mice coming together in a dance that said, "I don't believe you." He could understand that it was a difficult thing to believe when he heard himself say it, but it was a more difficult thing to see.

"And do you know where the dog is now, Mr. Cheevers?" the doctor asked, scribbling notes and trying to keep an eye on big Mr. Cheevers who stood, eyes closed, arms crossed and with his belly hanging over the front of the desk.

"Yes, well, no. My mother put the dog in the car and drove away, but I'm not sure where they went, I couldn't say. I haven't seen either of them since then, and that was three days ago, I think," he concluded, still speaking with his eyes closed.

"And you have been with us for those three days?"

"Yes. After she drove away, a coconut fell on my head and I woke up in the emergency ward and then I must have passed out again and I woke up just this morning."

"Hmm-hmm," said the doctor, the sailboat once again jiggling by the sunset.

Mr. Cheevers began rubbing the back of his head, remembering how much it had hurt when the coconut hit him. There was quite a lump there now—he could feel it under his hair.

"Thank you, Mr. Cheevers. I'll just get Miss Marshall to see you back to your room. He went to the door of his office and called to his receptionist, who bustled in and took Mr. Cheevers back to his room, which was down a windowless corridor, around a few corners, up an elevator and on the brightly lit fifth floor.

As they started walking, Miss Marshall had to guide Mr. Cheevers by the elbow because he refused to open his eyes, but after a time she assured him that if he did open his eyes no lightning bolts would penetrate, and if he thought they might, he could surely close them again. This made Mr. Cheevers more comfortable, the knowledge that he could be in charge of opening and closing his eyes, and after a few more steps he found he was even able to put his arms back down at his sides, and this felt much better. Then they made their way up to five and were greeted by welcoming plants and smiling staff.

Once back in his room, Mr. Cheevers tried to recall anything else at all about the blue car and the red book, but the recollection of screaming kept other memories from coming solidly into him. They cracked in his mind like fractured scraps—a glint here and there, a sliver of his mother's face, her screaming mouth, the dog, jumping up and catching the book in its mouth, and then a quick aural memory, just the hint of the loud noise that made him look up in time to see the coconut coming straight towards his head.

When he awoke the next day in a quiet and comfortable pale yellow room, he felt groggy and different. The screaming was out of his ears and his thoughts were clear and calm. He didn't feel anything urgent pressing on his brain, like a balloon pushing it to one side of his skull, and though he checked around in his mind, there were no thoughts that needed attention and this made Mr. Cheevers feel happy. He did have an unusual taste in his mouth, and he reached for the glass of water on his small bedside table.

"Good morning, Mr. Cheevers!" A smiling girl in a blue flowered top came in and handed him a small paper cup with two pills inside. "Oh, good. You've got your water already. Here you go." She stood while he put the pills in his mouth and washed them down with a sip of the tepid water.

Almost every day was the same: wake up, take pills, wash and dress, eat breakfast in the big dining room with everybody else, then group (which was in the same room, but with the tables pushed to the edges, sitting in a circle with all the same people and talking about yourself and how you felt with a doctor or nurse to lead the questions), then alone time (when in the beginning Mr. Cheevers would sit behind his bedroom door with his jacket over his head to stop the screaming), then lunch, then activities time, then rest, then dinner, then recreation, then ready for bed and finally sleep. After a while, Mr. Cheevers explored a bit more and slept a bit less. He no longer felt that he could only move sideways within a ten-meter semicircle of his room. He went even further, with no ill effect, and instead of spending activities time mostly on his own, he began talking to some of the other people and being interested in what was going on. He started playing chess in the recreation room and joined in with art class and the yoga, and he especially loved the gardening. He loved putting his hands into the soft brown soil, he loved the hope of growing things and his favorite place was outside on the small deck with some seeds and terracotta pots in front of him. In fact, he couldn't remember feeling so happy about anything.

The screaming had stopped during the day, but sometimes it was in his dreams and he woke up anxious. But when he opened his eyes, it stopped immediately, and Mr. Cheevers could tell the dreams from reality now. He'd be in bed; there would be a light on in the hall and somebody would walk by and ask if he was okay or needed anything. He knew the difference.

Three weeks later, Blake (as Mr. Cheevers liked to be called now— not so formal, he told the staff) was ushered down to the second floor, to the room with the receptionist and the chairs against the wall. Blake did not recall being in that room, or ever being in the doctor's office, so when he was handed the form, it was new to him and he filled it out, handed it back to the stout short-sighted receptionist, smiled at her and went to sit down. He picked up a magazine and leafed through it and was halfway through an article on the pyramids when he was shown into the inner room and then through the door into the doctor's office.

"Mr. Cheevers," the doctor said.

"That's me. Blake Cheevers." He smiled.

"How are you feeling?" the doctor asked, making a few notes as he spoke. Blake liked the sailboat floating in the pen.

"Really good," Blake replied calmly. The doctor read the form Blake had filled out.

"I see here that you work for the city," he said, putting the paper with its tiny writing down on the desk in front of him.

"Yes, at the recycling facility," Blake responded, and then answered all the doctor's questions.

"No family, no."

"Dating a waitress from the Denny's around the corner from your work?"

"Yes, Claudia."

"Bad dreams?"

"Sometimes . . . noisy dreams, but they stop when I wake up."

"And finally, Mr. Cheevers, do you know why you're here?" the doctor asked.

"I think it maybe has something to do with my dreams," Blake said, tentative.

"Yes, you had a psychotic break." The doctor explained what that meant and why it happened and how brain chemistry worked and why the medication was working.

"Will it happen again? Can I stop it?" Blake asked, concern rising in his voice.

"No, but as long as you continue on your medication and come to your appointments regularly, we can monitor you so it doesn't happen again."

Blake was satisfied and within a week he was released.

Being home didn't feel familiar, though. He recognized his apartment and his things, but he felt . . . detached from them. He walked around picking up this or that and felt nothing. He knew what his things were and their history: a signed baseball, he could recall the day he got it; his hockey gear stored in the closet, he remembered playing with his beer league team. But he felt no happiness in the memories, and Blake shut the closet wondering how he could get it back.

Since being home, he had spoken to Claudia on the phone a few times and explained what had happened as best he could. She was wary of him and they agreed to meet at Denny's after her shift.

"You did seem sort of excited all the time, and were getting sort of, uhm, bossy. Is that what was wrong?" she asked, recalling their last date when Blake had insisted it was safer for them to walk home backward.

Blake explained what he thought had happened and what the doctor had said, and Claudia sat listening, her burger getting cold in front of her. Blake had no appetite either, and they sat in silence picking at their French fries when he was finished his explanation.

"How do you feel now?" Claudia asked. She wasn't smiling, and Blake could see the wariness in her eyes.

"Good. I feel okay. I feel sort of sleepy all the time, but I don't have any dreams. But good—I feel steady." It was the only word he could come up with.

"Oh, that's good." Claudia looked down and removed her name tag from her shirt. "Well, I should probably get home." She zipped her backpack and signed the bill. "It's on me." She finally smiled.

As Blake watched Claudia get on the bus and wave out the back window, he felt the same about her as he did his hockey stick, which was not much of anything. He walked a few blocks over to his own bus stop and, while standing under the sign, he had a flash of memory, something about Claudia. He could remember ordering her around, telling her what to do, like he was her boss, not her boyfriend and he was happy to shut the door on that memory too. No reason to keep it.

Months later, Blake was still following the routines because routines help keep things in check. There were variations—a new psychiatrist that he met with every other week, and new exercises and diets and medications. But most importantly, there were the flower boxes on his balcony, which Blake had made in his shop class, and which he was filling and tending as he had learned in his gardening class.

Blake felt hopeful when he saw green emerge from the soil, and as the summer went on and the flowers matured, he even felt some joy and a bit of pride every day when he stood on the balcony with his watering can.

Good Planning

I don't care what they say, vermin are vermin. In fact, I think that's why they call them that name: ver-min. What else but something small and dirty and furry, things that live in the dank and make chattering noises. What else but something that would store away food for months and eat it all rotted. The problem has been going on for two years now, ever since I bought the place. At first, I could see them scamper across the grass, no wait, scamper denotes bunny rabbits which are close to vermin, but then I don't mind them too much. Vermin, they slink or skulk across the grass in the shadows and sometimes the big brazen ones cavort out there in midday. I see cars slow for them and wait patiently as they stand in the middle of the road unsure whether or not to cross. I could help them make up their minds. Their tiny pea-brain minds. There would be no question whether to cross or not cross if they skulked in front of my Impala. The answer would be: *no you will stay there on the road in a bloody pile in the hot sun offending children and old people until some too kind soul comes to scrape up your stinking carcass.* I blame the children and the old people actually, always feeding the vermin, always laughing and pointing and smiling at them as they stand there stupidly undecided whether to stop traffic or run up a tree for the precious nuts. Damn them anyway, it's all their fault really. I tried to bring it up with the town council at the last meeting and they didn't even respond, all those men in their suits and ties trying to look important like they had any more idea what they were doing than anyone else. Those mouth breathers. They just sat there listening to asinine complaints about pit bulls and ants and spraying in the neighborhood for moths, when in reality it is the vermin who are spreading the disease. Hadn't I myself been sick four times in the last year with unknown stomach complaints? It was the vermin all right. The vermin. But they hadn't listened, in fact they dismissed me. *Thank you for your concern Mr. Tebbs. We will look into it further if the situation warrants. Next!* I stepped down then but not after voicing my opinion further to the people sitting around me, but what good would that do, they were all the old people, the ones who like the vermin, like to feed them and take pictures of them. Sadists! It's you people who are bringing them into the neighborhood! I shrieked at them but they didn't care. They turned away and pretended not to hear just like the rest of the world. Give them a problem, offer them a crisis and what do they do? Just walk away until it becomes one of epic proportion. Meet with twenty-four different heads of state to decide what to do in a national state of emergency, but for God's sake surely you must not try to do something when the problem is small and manageable, that would be insane! Driving home from the hardware store today I could see the people pointing as I drove by. I could see them whisper to their children as I unpacked my purchases. Go ahead and laugh. Go ahead and point and stare, it's for your own good all of you! I yelled this silently at them so I would not arouse the vermin, but then dropped a bag full of rat traps and a glass jar of Planters peanuts. It smashed all over the driveway. Shit. I cussed too loud but then reeled myself in. Too loud, too loud! Keep calm, they can smell fear. Just pick up the nuts, every last one of them and slowly back yourself into the house I said to myself. I did that and it worked. I think. But no, there they are. They sensed me and they're up there now, in the attic, planning. God, it sounds like there are hundreds of them. When I stand silently, they stop, but when I make the slightest noise, right when they think I can't hear them, they start up again with their incessant chatter and their scurrying and skulking. Not only have they brought plague to this town, they have destroyed my house. My house. This house that I worked so hard to buy. Not everyone who bags groceries can afford a house but I scrimped and saved every penny, every tip from those damn people —"Can I carry your groceries to your car?" I'd ask, and it only took twenty years. Now that's planning my mom would've said, she would've been proud of me. My mom and my dad too maybe but he died when I was nine, then it was just me and my mom and she would be so proud of me. She knew I'd amount to something and she would have been so proud. I smiled and rested my arm on the fridge and drank a cold Coke and popped a few Planters into my mouth and spit a piece of bloody glass into the sink. Time to get to work. I can hear them now they had left for the afternoon. Planned it no doubt, it was my only chance it had to be today I could feel that the females were pregnant and I know that they can give birth to hundreds and thousands of them I know I've seen it on the nature channel. I know the damage they can wreak it can be an absolute disaster. But today I am prepared last year I wasn't last year I bought a few mouse traps and laced them with peanut butter and they just ate the peanut butter but didn't spring the traps I knew then that these were no average vermin in fact that's when I began to suspect that due to the proximity of the nuclear plant these vermin have evolved it was the only explanation. I can't believe that nobody will take me seriously especially in this town so close to the plant they're always talking about something happening dammit all the town lives in fear of danger people keep their children away from it. I think they're using it as an excuse for everything birth defects cancer madness I don't know everything but when there is one good idea one very good example of what has to happen not just hearsay but someone standing there with proof, they didn't listen *no why should they* it's too big it's just too big for this town to handle. That's why I started writing to the higher-ups when my first letter to the state health department was returned last year but that was only because I had the wrong address so I went to the library got the right one and now I write a letter every other day sometimes and sometimes every day. Last week I wrote to the White House and the Marines yes the Marines I thought it only fair that they be put on alert nobody else was going to do it almost getting to the point where the infestation could reach epic proportions but I haven't heard back from them yet and old man Jacobs down at the hardware store is starting to give me a hard time he's always asking what's this for what's that for *mind your own damn business* that's what I think geez if they're not gonna help and be supportive the least they can do is mind their own damn business *don't mix those* he says all the time as if he knows anything. They've started again I can hear them chattering probably making plans I think that they've actually developed their own language in fact after listening to the tape-recording I've made I'm sure of it. I sent it last week to the university linguistics department and just for safety to the FBI so if anything should happen to me they'll need to know they'll need to start planning for a counter-attack they'll need to have their labs start working on some antidote some antidote for the illness for the terrible illnesses that they'll bring like that kind I had last year when I was so sick I could barely move and couldn't see straight couldn't eat anything at all I've been poisoned by the vermin, been poisoned that's why I only eat rations now they're not bad you get used to it God knows that's probably what we'll all be eating soon anyway once they pollute the food supply God knows so I might as well get used to it now at least I'll be healthy though need help with the wounded, the walking wounded I can just imagine what it's going to be like carnage probably total devastation. They've stopped I have to get the trap set I have to mix the poison I only have a short time a small window they'll be back soon *damndamn-damn* look at what they've done to the attic it's worse than I thought I'll never know how they got back in they must of been hiding or tunneling and coming up the stairs while I slept it's the only explanation there is no way that anything could've gotten through the razor wire nothing would live nothing they would have had the furry flesh torn from their perky limbs savages coming in the night I picked up the razor wire on the internet the internet is really a good place to find things like this I want to find a recipe for explosives but I think I'll save that until needed I saved it to my favorites file but that will be a job for the Marines when they come if this doesn't work I did find a gun for now bought it online I love buying online I got an AK 45 I bought a magnum too I keep than that one with me at night right under my pillow I feel safer knowing it's there now that I know they've been in the house *nowthatIknow* they've watched me sleep that's why I don't sleep much these days I know they're laughing at me I

JENN ASHTON

can hear them now *snickersnicker* with their little furry tails jiggling with laughter and one night they nibbled my toes I know that's when I got sick well they can't laugh now can they I can hear them they're up there now by my calculations they should be extinct *inabouttenminutes* I can hear them now they're all eating *how nice of me to put food out* for them *haha* just like the children and old people yes it's true I'm such a good person *haha* well it's true my mother always said I was a really good boy better than the others even better than my own daddy she said and look at what I'm doing now practically saving humanity God I wonder what kind of award they can give somebody like me the highest honors I bet *can you hear them they've stopped I think that's it they're gone* I always carry the gun up with me just in case it's a trap good thinking my mother would say good planning and you have to climb up slowly it's better that way if you just run up and surprise them and God knows what would happen God knows they could maybe jump at you and eat *atyoureyes* with those teeth have you seen those teeth they grow and grow they say I read that in a book somewhere they just keep growing and they keep sharpening them I bet they don't tell the children that part well I know they don't *I tried to tell some children in the park once about the teeth and the fact that they might jump on their heads while they're sleeping and eat their eyes out the parents didn't like that much* it's a conspiracy *Ithinkitsallaconspiracy* they didn't even thank me for trying to help I hear them how can that be can you hear them scurrying around where's my flashlight damn they're still here I can hear them scurrying around my feet can you hear them damn this will fix them blast blast blast blast fucking squirrels they're gone now I think *atlastIdonthearthem* anymore I can hear some small noises but I think that's just the insulation in the wind with a few loose

118

shingles I'll have to get up there and fix the roof tomorrow there are a few holes but I don't hear them can you hear them I don't think they'll be back next year *ohfinallycanyouhearthe sirensfinally they're coming to help infestation must be muchworsethanIsuspected.*

Virginia, Ten

"Eccles cake, ECCLES CAKE!"

"Jimmy, repeating it and yelling it at me doesn't make me remember them any faster!" I turned and walked away, leaving my little brother staring at me. Of course I remembered the time Sylvia, our mother, had brought the cakes home as a surprise and we had loved them so much, their sweet crumbliness making a huge mess everywhere while she laughed, sort of hysterically.

I just liked fucking with Jimmy.

"You bitch." He swatted me as he passed me in the hall, and when I jerked away from his hand, I bashed my other shoulder into the wall.

"Ow!"

"Aw, I didn't even touch you," Jimmy mumbled. He shuts his bedroom door on the words.

I don't know why I treated him the way I did, we are always pushing and shoving each other and name-calling. "Sticks and stones" is my favorite line as Jimmy called me every name he could think of for pushing him over when he's bending down tying his shoes. Jimmy just feels like a pest and even though I know I should

121

be loving on him, he just gets on my every last nerve. Mr. Graves, my science teacher, would probably say it comes down the family in our genes. My mother is 'bipolar,' my father has been gone since I can remember and Jimmy's dad is in prison, for life, for killing his last wife. Even my grandparents are wacks, and we never see them. Maybe that's why I don't know how to love Jimmy like I should all the time.

Sylvia isn't home yet, so I go into the kitchen and grab a rice cake, then walk through the garage to the little room on the other side. We call it "the store" and it's full of stuff, like so much stuff you would think it was a Walmart. There are shelves lined with perfume and pencils and scotch tape and school duo-tangs, parakeet food (even though we never had one), bags of Halloween candy that have been there for years, shoelaces in every color, so many facecloths, and coffee cups and pink erasers by the box. On the floor there are full bags and boxes of stuff that have never been opened, just dumped there by Sylvia upon her return from one of her many shopping sprees.

Sometimes I liked to go stand in there and just look around. Sometimes I take something, like a book or some art paper, but mostly I just stand there and stare. It's the only place in the house where I feel like my mother is. When she is in one of her manic phases, she's kind and happy. When Mrs. Hyde takes over, it's a different story. She never comes out of her bedroom and I am fully in charge of Jimmy.

I mean, I'm in charge of him now anyway, but at least when she's manic she brings home some food and shops a lot. But when she goes dark, we never see her and I have to check on her like I'm her mother. "Is Sylvia good or bad today?" I ask her through a crack in her door. Sometimes there's a moan, but not usually, and if I can see the mess of blankets move up and down and I don't smell anything dead, I figure she's okay.

I've smelled dead stuff and I know what it's like. You probably think I'm making this all up but I'm not. Once we had a cat and it disappeared for days and I found it dead in the hedge beside the garage. I guess Sylvia had run it over. It didn't look like a cat anymore; it looked like it was made out of cardboard. It was stiff when I picked it up, but some of its fur was still soft and I stroked it and apologized for my mother's behavior. She didn't know any better.

That's how I know what dead smells like and so that's how I know Sylvia is okay: if it doesn't smell in there, she's okay. I hate these times actually and sometimes I sort of wish she would just die, then things might change and maybe we could get into care. I've heard good things, a few of the kids in my school are in care and word travels fast. Some of the foster families are super-nice and the parents buy you tons of stuff and new clothes to make up for your crappy other life, and there is always food and they make it for you and because they feel sorry for you there's hardly any chores. I've heard good things and bad things about being in care, but I'd risk a bad home if we had a chance at a good one. I wish that for Jimmy too, because I know I'm not a very good mother to him.

In fact, I hate being a mother. I mostly only know how to make mac and cheese from the blue box and we eat lots of cereal or microwave stuff when Sylvia remembers to buy it, and I feel bad when I see how scrawny Jimmy is, so I buy a bunch of junk from the corner store. He especially likes SweeTart Hearts, the kind with the sappy writing on them. Maybe he imagines I'm actually saying it to him when he makes me read them all: "You're my best pal," "I love you" or "Be mine Valentine." Anyway, it keeps him quiet and happy, even though I know it rots his teeth and he hates brushing. Sometimes I do it for him and I have to wrestle him to the ground, but it gets the job done. If I've been especially hard on the toothbrush, I take him into the room-off-the-garage store and let him get a new toothbrush and anything else he wants. His favorite thing is to go through the bags and play archaeology. He always comes up with something interesting, except the time he found a bag of used maxi pads.

"What's this?" he asked holding the bag up in the air.

"Put that down, Jimmy. They're Sylvia's personal things."

"Oh." He put the bag down carefully, and I made him wash his hands. He was respectful of her; he knew she was sick, even his teacher had told him that.

At school, the kids sort of leave us alone. I know we're not always clean, sometimes Jimmy won't stay still for me to wash his hair, and a lot of our clothes are too small. Once last year, my teacher gave me a pair of sneakers from the lost and found because mine were so old they were coming apart and my big toe poked out the top.

The teachers are super-nice to us because they know about my mother. There was this one time, when I was little and before Jimmy started school, Sylvia came in her big car to pick me up and she drove right up on the school grass and through the tulip garden we had all planted. She sat in her car honking and yelling that she had come to pick me up. Jimmy was in the front seat, not in a car seat or anything, and he was only two. Well, he wasn't in the front seat exactly, he liked to sit on the floor.

She looked like a full-on maniac and the principal, Mrs. Buchanan, ran out to see what had happened. She probably thought it was a horrible accident, but it was just Sylvia, who was one big accident all on her own.

My teacher wouldn't let me get in the car and the police came and took Sylvia to the hospital because they thought she was drunk. I heard one of the teachers whispering, and another teacher took Jimmy and I didn't see him until the next day. He must have gone home with Mrs. Palmer, the school secretary, that time, because I saw him with her in the morning, when Sylvia came to get him, like picking up a package from the post office. You could see she was on her way down.

That day Mrs. Buchanan drove me home, and even though I was really too little, she dropped me off at my house. I guess she thought there was somebody there to look after me, but there wasn't. I just let myself in with the key around my neck and grabbed a box of Pop-Tarts and watched TV until I fell asleep. I got up and went outside to wait for the school bus when I saw Jack Spicer, the weatherman from the morning news, was on. "Today's going to be sunny," I repeated to myself as I locked the door behind me.

Once they knew there was something wrong at our house, my teachers seemed more interested in me and even gave me food out of their own lunches and they always asked about Jimmy and sometimes gave me a bag of stuff to take home. Usually, it had like a bar of soap and sometimes a pack of socks or underwear. I didn't know how to do laundry then, but now I do.

I feel pretty grown-up that I figured out how to work the washer and dryer all by myself. I like laundry days actually, making the clothes clean, like today when I grab the pile of clothes from Jimmy's bedroom floor and there's this smear of blueberry jam and the big splash of chocolate milk down the front of his red and white striped t-shirt; it's a real mess, but the messier the better—I love the challenge. It's his favorite t-shirt and I know I can get it looking clean. All the stuff usually comes clean again.

When Jimmy's a bit taller, I'll teach him to do the laundry too.

Mecca

Every year my Great Auntie Kay and Great Uncle Hank make the trip up to Mecca, Saskatchewan, to breathe in one of the new babies. Auntie Kay sits in the hospital and rocks them and hums Sunday School songs, and Uncle Hank sits in a chair opposite in his reeky old coveralls, his knobbly, arthritic hands on his knees, and beams at them.

It was the same routine every time and I had witnessed it every year for as long as I can remember, because if there is one thing this family is good at, it's breeding.

As I was about to leave for home, leaving my new cousin in the care of her greats, a familiar man walked up to me. He was young, wore glasses with thick red frames, and I knew him as Just Jack, one of the hospital social workers. He would buzz in and out of our homes to check on the new arrivals after a few weeks or so, him or one of the other workers, May or old Sharon who walked with sticks because of polio. Mostly now it was him though, and the kids would yell, "It's just Jack" from the front window when the doorbell rang.

He walked up to me and asked if we could chat. I know I rolled my eyes.

"Okay," I said, and we moved to some chairs away from Kay and Hank, but not far enough away that we couldn't still hear the humming.

"I heard you spoke with the school counselor about some thoughts you were having?" he said, getting right down to it.

"It's nothing," I said

"Well, it sounds like something," Just Jack said. "What's up, wanna talk about it? You're important, you know, and I want to help if I can." He smiled at me.

"Well, it's not every day your mom goes bankrupt!" I blurted. I guess I got right down to it too. I could feel the sad coming up my throat and strangling me a little bit. I hadn't wanted to blurt that out, it just came out of nowhere and I could feel my cheeks flushing. It was always at the tip of my brain now, and I guess it was on the tip of my tongue too because out it shot.

"Yeah, but it has nothing to do with you," he said matter-of-factly. "Your mom's business is her business and your business is being her kid and doing the school thing."

I stared at him again. He had no idea what it was like to be a kid in this family. Bankruptcy meant public and private shaming. It meant trips to the bank, papers to sign and me, as the oldest, helping my mom close up the shop while she tried to figure out the computer and start an online Etsy store. It meant that, ready or not, I was the one who sat at the kitchen table when she cried, bringing her coffee and Kleenex, and it was me who went with her to the single-parent meetings in the basement of the church every Tuesday night.

If Just Jack could see behind my cold stare, he'd know all that.

"I'm fine," I said to my winter boots, and he slapped my knee.

"Okay. Well, you know you have a herd of people dying to talk to you if you need it," and he embraced the almost empty waiting room with his arms wide and we both laughed as I got up to leave.

"Hang on a sec." He waved me back into the chair and he went down the hall to the row of black vending machines, pulled some change out of his pocket and fed it into the closest one. He came back smiling, with a white cardboard cup with a little pink plastic stir-stick in it and handed it to me. "For the walk home. Decaf."

"Thanks." I shook my head—they were all about decaf, always trying to swap it to us kids as if we didn't know the difference. Then he saw the boy and grinned.

"Oh, hey, Louis!" He yelled to a tall, skinny kid standing in front of the elevator while I blew on my coffee.

"Come over and meet Louis, Jess. He can walk you home." He took my elbow to escort me over to the elevator.

"Hey, Jack," the kid, Louis, said with an accent.

"Hey, Lu, meet Jess. You're both here welcoming new family members today, and I thought you could walk Jess home. She's on your way." Just Jack started to walk backward towards the waiting area.

"Hi," I said, raising my cup to Louis.

"Hi." He smiled and I could see how white his teeth were. "Sure, yeah, no problem, Jack."

"So . . . great!" Jack gave us a thumbs-up as he backed away and left us standing by the elevator.

"So, are you ready to go?" Louis asked, pointing to my coffee.

"Yeah," I said, and the kid pressed the down arrow button beside the elevator and we waited, both staring uncomfortably at the old patterned pink and blue wallpaper I knew so well.

When we were outside in the cold it seemed easier to talk, and we talked to keep warm. I didn't live far from the hospital, but it was nice to walk with somebody, and in the short distance home I found out that Louis was also the oldest, came from another family that was good at breeding, and was fluent in Spanish. Once I discovered that, we spoke only Spanish for the remainder of the walk, his beautiful and lilting, and mine broken and hesitant, but it worked, and by the time we reached the door to my apartment building, we were what kids' books call "fast friends."

It was coming up to the end of November and holiday plans were being made. Emily was over trying to talk my mom into her idea of renting a hall this year for a grand Christmas buffet, but my mom was too involved with her laptop to be in that conversation, and she mostly just answered "mmhmm" to Em's questions.

Holidays for our family meant traveling around Mecca and to neighboring towns, trying to see as much family as we could squeeze in. Only families with the freshest babies were exempt from traveling. It was a busy and frantic time and involved a lot of cooking and eating. For us kids, it wasn't a big deal, the visiting part, because we all saw each other in school every day anyway.

I could hear Em counting at mom as she made her case for the hall, " . . . and that's just the dads and the kids alone, and that's already fifty-one people!" she said, her voice getting higher at the end of her sentence as she looked at me wide-eyed and exasperated. I just shrugged my shoulders at her. That's usually the look they get in their eyes when they marry into this breeder family, the numbers alone are often overwhelming.

Emily was my cousin Jim's wife, and she came from a family with just two kids, her and her older sister. Holidays in her family, from what I had gathered in our previous conversations, meant getting dressed up in your newest clothes and driving a few blocks away, to sit sedately in your grandparents' houses, wondering why they had fake Christmas trees, and eating once-a-year sweets and fancy baking. It meant quietly wandering around empty halls, running your hands along the paint and tiles, bored to tears in too-tight patent leather shoes, while you waited for your parents to finish talking so you could drive around and look at Christmas lights displayed on your neighbors' houses for ten minutes before you went home. The quiet home which I imagined would be as echoey as a school gym when nobody was there, with shiny clean floors and all that s p a c e.

I glanced from Emily to the mudroom floor, which was holding up very well considering there were almost always eight pairs of wet, snowy and muddy boots, and a hundred kilos of various skis, sleds and clothes in a heap on it.

We were learning about contrast in art class and I can imagine how she feels, Emily, coming into this family, the contrast between her old life and her new life. Her stark and quiet, prim and proper, blue-sky sunny days West Coast life picked up and thrown into the dark and snowy vortex when she took hold of Jim's hand. Where once her ideas were worthy and fluid, now she came to stand inside this box here in Mecca with the rest of us, squeezed in so tightly that we couldn't change positions if we wanted to.

And they would never work here, her ideas. She could maybe convince Jim, and he might be able to convince one or two of his brothers or their wives, but in the end, it would be a handful against a mountain. The sheer numbers would make it an impossible thing to do. She might as well be trying to move that mountain with a garden trowel. Sadly, her only hope of gaining support in this family was to start having babies or leave the province, but even then, Jim would be obliged to come back for holidays and that would just mean a longer, more expensive trip. So they would stay and she would get absorbed into the rest of us, helpless. But at least she would have her memories, and I would love to have her memories. I've imagined a life like hers: pretty and still, having quiet places to read and things that are all your own.

Then the twins were there, asking me to get down the big bag of flour so they could practice their cookie recipe for 4H, so I left off watching the exasperated Emily and went to carry the twenty-pound bag of flour out of the pantry to the kitchen table.

I liked her hall idea though, and I could imagine the freedom of it: being able to come in and talk with whoever you wanted, eat whatever you wanted, stand wherever you wanted and most importantly, leave whenever you wanted. It sounded easy enough, but it would just be impossible getting everybody on board. Things don't change much here.

All-Nation Soup

My granny used to make this thing called "all-nation soup." It was basically hamburger soup but it had four kinds of beans in it. I think she just made it up from what she had. We had it every Sunday at her house, when all of our parents dumped us off there, to go and do whatever they did on a Sunday afternoon. I'm pretty sure it was not to go to church. I think my mother went to work and my father to the bar, or maybe they all just went back to bed, happy to be rid of us for a few hours.

All of the cousins would be there, the aunts and uncles driving up in a queue outside the old apartment block, some nodding to each other from the driver's seat, and others hungover and ignoring everybody. We would all rush up to the glass doors with the big words Regent Manor in gold writing; it was always a race to see who could push the buzzer and then we'd lean against the dirty white stucco and feel the sharp glass pieces through our t-shirts, jean jackets and windbreakers and wait for granny to buzz us in. The first thing we would do was huddle in the kitchen and watch granny stir the soup pot and start to build up that soup. The dank smell of beans, when the pot reached a boil, would hit our noses before she put the other ingredients in.

"That's the way it's done," she'd say. "You have to start with nothing and build it into something, that's where the magic is. First, you have nothing, then you have something!" and she would wave her wooden spoon with a flourish, like a wand, and smile her gummy smile, her grey perm bobbing as she laughed while she slowly moved around the small kitchen, the arthritis already having taken a firm hold of her small, stout sixty-five-year-old frame. We had heard different versions of this every Sunday for as long as I can remember, but Granny's lessons were never boring, and usually combined a recipe of some sort with a bit of family history and most times a moral tacked on the end, "just to keep us pure."

Now that I'm grown up, I know how long she must have spent making that soup for us, because beans take a long time to make. I know she must have had patience and so much love for us to make that special thing for all of us kids every Sunday.

We would all roll in, ten of us more or less, and get dumped off around two or three in the afternoon. We'd kind of bum around until supper time, when we would all sit around the old table. Granny would have put the leaf in before we arrived, just in case our full count of fifteen ever showed (we never did except at Easter, Christmas and her birthday), and she always put on a nice, freshly pressed linen tablecloth for us and we got to use the good old-fashioned roses china, and the forks and knives out of the locked wooden box from the bottom of the china cabinet.

"Special things should be used every day because every day is special," she would remind whoever was helping her set the table that day. We would always fight over who got to help her with the preparations; it felt grown-up to do things like fold and smooth the white napkins. Reverent.

Now that I know that's how they do it in a fancy restaurant, I know that Granny was trying to make us all feel special, and we did, even though sometimes we didn't know it at the time. Sometimes Bill kicked us under the table, and Roger always had a drippy nose and didn't care what he ate, the steam just made his nose run more. Anne Marie was always reading, but she'd put down her book when Granny would go around the table holding the big pot with her green checked tea towel, ladling the soup for us, and her bowl was full. Granny served that soup like it was her only job, and we were kings and queens, not just grubby kids. She radiated love at us, and it was sometimes the only soul food we got all week. Most of our parents worked and that meant that us older kids were left to fend for ourselves for supper and most of the younger ones were on a regular diet of frozen TV dinners which were then all the rage. When I look back now, I'm sure that these warm and caring Sundays with Granny were what kept us all going in the swiftly evolving seventies, where families were no longer like the Waltons we saw on TV but were instead a minefield of changing ideas and ideals.

Granny saw in us what we didn't during that time—our potential. She came from a time when there wasn't much, when war raged and you were just happy to have your family home safe and a bit of food on your table. I found out much later that Granny didn't have all of that for long, that she had lost children to smallpox and siblings in that war and to Spanish Flu and so she loved us all extra hard. She came from a time of hugs and kisses, when mothers were always home and you had all of their care and attention for the rest of their lives, when children were prized and family came before all else, and now she witnessed us living in a world of broken homes and hard words. So there were no harsh words there, no "sit up straight" or "why are you making that face" or "wait till your father gets home" or "eat everything on your plate or else." Instead there was just a relaxing in, an unspoken conversation of sorts between us and her, where we all felt like royalty sitting at her table, where she listened to us talk and modeled good behavior and had us in stitches holding our sides at least once during every meal when she related family stories from her day: Grampa driving the first trolley cars or great-granny working in the hardware store. We hung on every word. The cold world outside stopped and we could breathe at Granny's table and just be ourselves.

Some grannies knit sweaters, but I think ours stitched us back up when we needed it, and stitched us together with her weekly soup pot. The legumes' protein helix wove around and through us, traveling to each child on the steamy ladle, tying us up tight and delivering us to a new week, happy with a bow on top, in the exact place where she kissed the top of each of our heads when she went around the table, passing out warm crackers and rolls, telling each one of us how much she loved us.

You could put the smell of Granny's soup in my nose a million miles away and I would be right back at that table, with all of my cousins. We are still tied that tightly, all these years later. Still, every time I watch the beginning of Walt Disney with my kids at six o'clock on a Sunday, I am transported back to my grandmother's bed, with its slippery green and gold bedspread, all of us piled on top together watching TV and then, as if drugged and warm, we would all start to nod off as Lawrence Welk or *Hymn Sing* came on. We would shiver at the voices and some of us would hum with the choirs even though we never knew the words, and Anne Marie could harmonize with the long-held notes. Then one by one we would fall asleep or drift into a sort of trance, maybe staring at the wooden plaque that held all of Granny's little spoons in its pride of place just outside the bedroom door, where she too could gaze happily at its shining contents from her bed. Her collection from travels, back when she was young like us. She took great care of them and they were always clean and never tarnished. Just like she took care of us.

It was a respite there at Granny's, on those Sundays from our regular lives of being cold and wet, walking back and forth to school, our jeans heavy and soaked to the knees, coming home to cold, empty houses almost every day when our parents were at work or just "out"; coming in when there was nobody home to turn the heat on or to tell us to get out of our wet clothes. Granny's apartment at Regent Manor was our little piece of heaven, that place that grew in its preciousness with each passing year even after Granny had gone on and all of the cousins had moved away. I am sure each of us bring out that memory every Sunday, wherever we are.

I've tried to make that soup for my family, but I can't get it right. I have tried about a hundred times, but I still can't get it. I think what my recipe is missing is the air back then, with all of our cousins' breath together in that small third-floor apartment, or maybe the ingredients were just different. Maybe it's missing the scent of our granny—Clorets and Listerine, Oil of Olay and peppermints.

The Weatherman

You know when you've read a book many times, and the characters and their names live in your mind's ear, but when you say those names and words out loud, suddenly they are strange and unfamiliar, the syllables jumbled and foreign? Out of the page and your head, they have no context and this world isn't theirs. That's how it was the first time I told Yuki, my wife, about the wind.

Words, now unfamiliar and sounding so strange and alien that I had to pause and make sure that I was actually pronouncing them correctly. My pulse raced, and I had to fight to keep down the excitement in my voice. I am a calm man. Once I won a fair-sized chunk of money on the lottery and waited three days to claim it, strolling to the bank at a leisurely pace. In emergencies people look to me for direction, but in relating my thoughts and findings to Yuki, I became a six-year-old boy on Christmas morning, so excited to finally pull off the wrapping paper.

Yuki stared at me when I was finished speaking. She stood up, kissed my forehead and went back to the kitchen where she had been cubing tofu for soup.

I watched her back as she worked. I knew she was thinking,

considering what I had told her. Things had to steep in Yuki's mind, just as they had to ripen in mine. Until she offered a response, I knew I could not speak to her again. I stood up from my chair and moved closer. I sat on a stool in the kitchen and watched her chop vegetables and place the soup pot on the stove. I could almost hear the information turning over in her mind, and I could see her jump a bit when a breath of wind came in through the sliver of open window and blew an onion skin across the chopping board, which she then stared at as if waiting for it to do something else.

"The wind," I heard her say to herself.

She scraped the last of the miso paste from a small jar.

"The wind."

Her face was still.

Tap, tap, tap. The spoon against the side of the old copper-bottomed pot.

The wind.

I could see her mind working. I could see that she was putting it together, piece by piece. It had to fit in Yuki's way.

She had been this way since she was a child. Things had to fit in her own special way. Yuki's father was the first to tell me how her mind worked.

He told me about when she was ten years old and she could not understand math. It was the early seventies and the advent of new math as well as the change from Imperial to metric, from Fahrenheit to Celsius. Yuki was failing math, despite tutors and hours at the table with her father. Then one day he spotted her in the garden trying to put the petals of a pear blossom in order, to make the blossom whole again. The pear blossom gave him an idea. He called Yuki to the table and laid her math book before her.

Mr. Oshima always laughed when he said how Yuki's big brown fawn eyes filled with tears as she looked at the textbook. But instead of methodically going through the formula with her, he simply gave her the answers. Her face changed then, he said, and it lit up like a bright midday. That day Yuki went through the entire math book as if her mind were a calculator, because once she had the answer, she was able to go backward through the question to see how it worked. She could piece it together backward like a mystery novel. There was no stopping her after that and she devoured her maths and even jumped ahead a few grades.

This is how Yuki's mind works. The mind of an artist, seeing the whole before the parts.

I knew what she needed was time, she needed to find a way to put the petals together. What I had just told her was not an easy thing to comprehend. Much bigger than new math.

I first met my wife when I was a child taking piano lessons from her mother. I would ride my bike to their house every day after school, and for an hour and a half be in my own kind of heaven.

Mrs. Oshima was a very kind and patient woman and would always feed me tea and biscuits and ask how my day had been before we ever sat at the piano. My audience was a small, slight girl who would stand and watch me play and clap when I was done, even just scales. Yuki was only four when I began my piano lessons there, and I stayed for three years until I went to high school and it was too far to bike.

I lost track of Yuki for years and did not meet her again until I was traveling in Scotland after college. There weren't many Japanese people in Dundee at the time, so it was not difficult to notice each other when we both stood waiting on the train platform heading to Aberdeen.

I would've recognized her if she had only been that pair of eyes. They spotted me, smiled and that was it. We married as soon as we got back to Vancouver and have been about the happiest couple of people that I've ever seen.

It hasn't always been a cliché of happiness, sweetness and light. We were poor and we both worked so many jobs to help each other through graduate school that we barely saw each other. Yuki's mother passed away soon after we were married, and we tried to persuade Mr. Oshima to come and live with us, but it was in vain, because he would never leave his garden. So he stayed in his too-big North Vancouver house, even after we left and moved to the island.

Years later, when her father died, Yuki packed up that entire house, not wanting to part with any of it, and moved everything here to the lighthouse with us, as if keeping all of her father's belongings close kept him here on this earth. They had a special understanding, father and daughter, and for most of her life Yuki said that not many people could understand the way her mind worked. Until she met me, of course.

"Smell this!" she would say, handing me his trowel with the wooden handle. "Can you smell it? Sandalwood and roses." She stuck the old trowel into the potted ivy on the kitchen sill, as if by planting it there, the man would grow back.

I had been working as an architect downtown and Yuki as a social worker in East Van. They were good jobs and we were happy, but we couldn't see ourselves staying in the city forever. Vancouver was growing, and we mourned the old city and gentle times when kids would rather bike to piano lessons after school than stay inside watching TV or playing games on screens. So we applied to work in a lighthouse during the time when the lighthouses were being automated. The government decided to keep a few of them manned, however, and we were lucky to get the position to run one. We didn't think it would last and we did not expect it to, but we are still here now all of these years later and still the happiest people that I've ever seen.

The work is not difficult, and one part of my job is to monitor and record the weather, marine and land, on our tiny island. I didn't understand why, in this age of satellite weather, but I guess they needed a human in the equation somewhere, and this little Japanese man fit the bill. Yuki has time to give painting classes at the small community center and for a while, I used to fish in the little stream a few miles inland and learned how to tie flies, but then I became interested in the weather.

The day came when I realized that I had been standing for hours, watching the trees move or that I was staring at the ripples on a still bit of river for even more hours, my fishing gear untouched. I knew then that some other purpose had entered my mind, and so my fishing gear was put away, indefinitely.

The lighthouse where we live is a mixture of old and new. The working part, which is at the top of the structure, is filled with the most modern and expensive equipment the government could afford to have out here. I've purchased more over the years, but mostly for my own studies. Even though the walls are a good foot or so thick and very sturdy, when you are up top, you can feel the wind push against the lighthouse, as if it were trying to get in, or trying to tell me something. I can disappear up there for hours, but Yuki doesn't mind.

Our home is in the base of the lighthouse. As an architect this made sense to me, like a snail that carried its shell on its back, the concentric circling stairs, a perfect Lasdun spiral, it all made sense in my mind that we were the nucleus. A few years after we arrived here, we were offered money to build an adjoining house, but both Yuki and I felt that if we were to live and work here, we needed to actually be a part of that space, we needed to be the living, breathing part of it. So we stayed in the base and put the money in the bank.

Had you not known that neither of us had ever been to Japan, you would think that we were longing for our homeland. Our home is filled with almost everything Yuki's father had kept, all of which had been from his family in Osaka. It has a sparse and traditional feel that is reflected in Yuki's paintings, the cedars made up of long and bold strokes and the eagle with the salmon in its claw was black, like ink on rice paper.

Yuki's easel stood in the middle of the kitchen, and books mixed in with pots and pans and bamboo steamers. There were a lot of books and we put them wherever they could fit. And in the living room, off to the side, is our Japanese bath. Yuki and I have spent many hours in that bath, talking and making plans. I think that is where we are most comfortable, and I guess that's why that night, as we soaked, she spoke her first words to me in more than four hours.

"Do you mean to say that the wind has evolved?" She stroked my left arm with a loofah sponge. "Are you trying to tell me that the wind has come alive and has developed emotion?" Her hands now lifting the warm water over my arm and washing away the soap.

"I'm not sure," I said, shaking my head. "I'm not sure about any of it. I don't know if it has come alive so much as it is a carrier of emotion. I don't know how, I don't know, but I can show you. Tomorrow, I'll show you," I promised her.

The bath lasted a lot longer, but not the discussion. We often lost track of time in the evenings, as our lovemaking seemed to fill every crack between the bricks and made the lighthouse live. We laughed when we first came here, that it was because of us that the light shone so brightly and that we were the makers of the waves that crashed on our shore.

Now it was Yuki who sat on the kitchen stool, and I stood before her trying to explain myself again. She's a patient woman my wife, one of the things I love most. She puts up with me.

"Yuki, do you remember sometimes when we were young we would stand and feel the wind and I would say to you, "This is the breath of a boy collecting seashells on the beach in Tanzania, or this is the breath of a mother giving birth in a hut in the countryside of Vietnam two hundred years ago. Think of that. And then think that somehow, like electricity or ions clustering, imagine that these emotions have clustered and stuck and made the wind thick with their presence. And imagine that now, when the wind comes and calms, imagine that those emotions are breathed into a population. It shares some concepts with biometeorology, but goes one step further."

"I think I see, Tekki, but how can it be? People have their own emotions. How can you say it's from the wind?" she asked, her chin resting on her fist, which rested on her thigh.

"Because it's not just one person having an emotion, Yuki," I said, cupping her face in my hands, her silver-brown hair whispering over my fingers. "It's an entire community, experiencing the same emotion at the same time.

145

"It's as if the time has come and the air is at last saturated with feeling. So much feeling!" I threw my hands in the air and moved them all around me, "Throughout time, the air has been quietly collecting our expressions, our vocalized emotions, and now it's giving them back in a lump, to people in places where the wind comes in and suddenly dies. Like here, Yuki, in our little town, and along the mountains and in Vancouver and everywhere in the world I would imagine; after a storm, or when the winds stall, too heavy to continue. Like in the summer you know, in the city. One minute there would be a nice ocean breeze, the next, stillness and heaviness. It used to amaze me that you could actually watch the mood of the people change. They would become angry and aggressive. I've read that violent crime spikes during a heatwave, that people are just cranky in the heat of summer, but no, do you see? It was the beginning of the emotional winds, not the greenhouse effect. It was already here, all of those years ago." I stood over her now and held her shoulders, "Yuki, it's even in you," I said quietly. "I've watched it happen."

"Have you spoken about this to anyone?" She asked me, her paint-stained hands wrapped around each other anxiously. "Do you have proof?"

"No, nobody knows and, yes, I think I have proof. Yes, I think so." Yuki's hands relaxed.

"I don't think I've lost my mind just yet, come on." I took her hand and led her up the spiral stairs, past the loft and into the working area of the lighthouse. "I want you to see this, it's not much, but I think it's directly related."

There aren't many windows down in the living area, so when we crave more light, we come up here. The windows offer a 360° view and, on a clear day, you can see Mount Baker. The glare could be too much at times, though, especially if the sun was shining in on the old brass fixtures, but today was a dull day and it was just white light.

Recording the weather statistics took about as much time as tying my shoes, and after I became computer literate, there was not much else to do up here but invent projects to work on. This project though, presented itself quite plainly to me, and although I do not keep anything from Yuki, I waited to tell her about this until I was sure. I knew how her mind worked and I knew I needed to give her the answer before all of the pieces.

It is not that she was not interested in my work, but Yuki is an artist and finds little amusement in technology. It was one of the things I admired about her. She held fast to her values and beliefs, that's why I knew this would be a challenge. I wanted her to believe me. I wanted her to be with me on this, on all levels. I knew that she would support me as a friend and as a partner, but with this, I needed more than her support, I needed her belief.

I sat her down in front of the computer screen and punched up some data that I had recently put together.

"Before you ask why someone else has not seen this, let me tell you that I think I'm the only one that has been looking at this data. I may be the only one that has been watching these trends, in this way. All of this data is usually sent off to computers to be dealt with before it ever reaches a human eye, but I see it as it comes in before it's sent off for compilation. A computer would miss what I am seeing, and any other person would ignore these changes if they didn't know what they were looking for or have the correlating data that goes along with it."

"What correlating factors are you talking about, Tekki?"

"It all started as fun, and I only began looking at the data in earnest when things started to make sense. So far, by putting these winds up against events in the news and by things I've witnessed, I've mapped at least four emotions and their responses." I handed her a spiral-bound notebook. I had been keeping notes and dates and times and events and it also contained my password for the computer data I had stored.

"Tekki, this is all little much for me to take in. Walk with me to town. I need a new cad red." She was speaking about paint colors, and I nodded and brought the notebook downstairs and left it on the kitchen counter. We put on our fleece and shells and left the lighthouse, the pages of the book opening and closing in the wind like a breath as we closed the door.

Yuki and I are the only couple that I know of that still hold hands when we walk. We strolled the mile into town in silence and went into the general store, run by the McNeils, who, like us, had left city living for a dream and were our close friends. Their son, Colin, yelled at us from the floor behind the counter, "What can I do for you all today?"

"Colin, what are you doing down there?" I peered over the counter only to see the back of his old Grateful Dead t-shirt and his bleached white jeans.

"I was changing the strings on my guitar and lost one of my bridge pins down in between his floorboards. No big deal really but it will be ages before I can replace it . . ." his voice became suddenly silent and I could hear him breathing intently as though he may just have it in his fingertips.

Yuki walked in from the back with the small tube of paint and a tin of peaches in her hand.

"Ah-ha! Holding out on us!" she waved the peaches in the air.

"Anything else for you guys?" He said as he smiled and pulled out a black ledger from underneath the counter and noted down the paint and peaches on the page.

"No, that's all I think," Yuki said coming to stand up against me. "We've got to run, Colin, we'll be back in a day or two."

We stood for a moment at the foot of the road and looked out over the water. There was a small breeze and Yuki looked at me quizzically.

"You said you had seen it in me?" she asked.

"Yes, I admit you are part of the experiment." I kissed the tip of her nose and she put her arms around me and spoke into my jacket.

"Is it really visible? I mean do I become somebody else? Do I get really bitchy or something? How do you know it's not just me and my moods?" Her questions came fast now, spilling out like somebody had released a cork from her mind after giving it a bit of a shake.

"No, no, it's not like that. In fact, it's very subtle in you." I was surprised at how well Yuki was taking this. It's not many people who would stand lovingly in your arms while you told them that the feelings that they were experiencing were not their own. But I knew Yuki would not think I was invalidating her feelings. I think it is because she knew or at least was beginning to have a small understanding of the phenomenon, which was occurring around us like an emotional contagion, moving from person to person, through a photograph or words spoken on the other end of the phone. From a voice sent on the wind, like a cloud, ready to burst, a collection of curses, the bad moods catching more than the good. We were being shown our greater connections, our interrelatedness to all others, the oneness that the Zen Buddhists already knew, the fact that we all "inter-are."

"And tonight's low includes a pile of bad moods swinging east over the mountains, don't get swept up in it!" Yuki laughed. Then she stood behind me, wrapping her arms around my waist.

Gusts of wind blew in off the harbor, but the dullness left the day. I think it was because of Yuki. She lights up the sun, and the gulls circled over us as if they were her halo.

Mea Culpa

My self-awareness appeared early and made me feel like there was something wrong with me. It also led me to always feeling left out of the conversation, like when my parents failed to consult me before having another baby, or when they decided we should move. I knew, too, when I had been wronged and treated unfairly, and I learned early on how to hold a grudge. I would have made the perfect little hitman.

A prime example would be kindergarten. This is when my first grudge came about, and I held it firmly against my chest, my teacher and many of the girls in my class when I had to take the fall for the cohort on my first day. I had walked into this room thinking I was pretty special because my grandfather had built the church the kindergarten was housed in, but I was in for a shock.

I stood in the back watching the other girls play, too shy to come forward and pick up a toy and join in myself, it all seemed kind of silly. In the back of the room there was a massive blue dollhouse and it was the thing to be playing with, even the boys took seats to watch the girls pretend. But when recess was over and everybody else ran away, I wasn't sure what the bell meant and I stood there feeling everybody push past me, back to the big rug where we were to gather for our next lesson. As I stood there, the teacher reprimanding me in front of the entire class for not cleaning up the dollhouse, I decided this school thing pretty much sucked.

The next day I played at going to school, but instead crouched down beside our front door and waited and picked at the peeling varnish, shivering in my leotards and little green coat with the fur collar. My plan was to wait there until I saw the other kids pass by on their way home. A short time later, when the mailman walked up our stairs, surprised to see the small girl crouched on the porch, I put my shush finger to my lips, nervous that he would tell on me.

He nodded, but to this day I am sure he gave me away, because that night my father sat me down on the piano bench and gave me a sort of lecture about lying.

Life is hard when you're four, and I already knew that I was off to a bad start with authority.

Why, you may be asking yourself, is she telling me all of this? The reason is this precisely: I have had such a great self-awareness, I have always known what I was doing, there was always a plan, so I could always be in charge, and in turn, could always take care of myself.

As a result, most of the time I have also been the one on the receiving end of discipline and punishment, and never in my life has anybody ever said, "I'm sorry." Even when what happened or what was done to me was so clearly somebody else's fault. I just didn't happen to grow up in that culture; as a rule, children were not apologized to.

So, in turn, I have never said "sorry" much either. Not with any real conviction or authority over the words at any rate. I have said it many times out of fear, or to stop a silly fight, (and I will always try to say it first in that circumstance because I read somewhere that it is the best thing to do). And although in the latter example it is always heartfelt, I don't feel like I have ever apologized to the right person for the right thing at the right time. So being that I am now the person I want to be, I'm going to take care of that oversight here.

I'm writing because I want to tell you about the last stupid thing I'll ever do. My life has been a series of stupid things, judged not only by me but by others as well. From putting myself into awkward situations to telling lies that have chased me through my life, to being so strangled by my fears that I forgot how to listen to my gut and my own intuition. The blackened hand that reached up to grab my throat wasn't real of course, but it was real enough to send me startled into the kitchen for a glass of juice at 3:00 a.m. At thirty-five you would think that summer-camp-fireside scary stories would no longer give me nightmares, but they did. And so did my lifelong fear of bears, earthquakes, floods and Godzilla (who would walk down my street in the middle of the night). And then there's Stephen King, but let's not even go there because I am just learning to sleep with the lights off.

Boris, not his real name, first came into my life a few years ago when the light above my dining room table started to smoke. Okay, I will also say that maybe I had installed it myself, all the time my now infamous gut telling me to hire somebody to do it properly, and even the Ikea instructions themselves might have mentioned it, but well, I just did it myself anyway. I can't remember how I came to find his card in my huge pile of cards, one of the stacks of things I randomly keep around my house, like unfinished knitting, unread magazines and brochures for local sights I'll never visit. I am just going to assume it ended up in my mailbox one day, even though my mailbox had a red dot on it indicating "no junk mail please!" And in the beginning I was so thankful to have found an electrician that I liked (and could afford) because my house was almost a century old, and the wiring had not been updated since the war. So, there he was, Boris the Bulgarian Electrician. (Not his real name, let me state again, because I do not want this dude to ever find me, and the card did not say Bulgarian either, I just added that because after I met him, I found out he was Bulgarian. End of rambling explanation.)

It was a white card with red writing and a picture of some wire and a plug and when you flipped it over it had a picture of a red desk lamp which was shining on his slogan, "So good it hertz," which seemed charming when I read it, but in hindsight maybe should have set off some fireworks in the gut area, especially after I met him.

When Boris arrived at my house in his dark brown van which he had customized himself, (as he proudly showed me an hour later as I walked him out), I could see by the look on his huge stony face that he meant business. That and his t-shirt, which he had also personalized himself and that said in big black lettering across the back, "Fuck Off I'm Working." That t-shirt and his sturdy frame alone gave me a bit of a thrill and then later a bit of a shudder. Even though he was only a few inches taller than my five-foot-four frame, he looked more like a very fit bull than a man. I would not have looked twice if he had taken off his dirty white ball cap to reveal a pair of horns.

So those were my initial thoughts. I thought he liked me okay, because we talked a lot about so many different topics from computer programming to university, to immigration and his experience, and I thought he was pretty smart and savvy. He was like some sort of Bulgarian mystic, if such a thing exists. I loved his stories and the way he spoke; I was his fan club and couldn't wait for a fixture to start smoking or for a breaker panel to need fixing. He had a gruff way about him but it was sort of commanding and you wanted to do things for him, like bring him water and invite him to dinner. Which I did, once; he shook his head and smiled and said, "No, you do not want to know me. I am a bad man." I laughed at his response, but his dark, slate-colored eyes bored into me and I knew that I probably should just do whatever it was he said, including not getting to know him better.

When he left after rewiring my old electrical panel, I tried looking him up on the internet. He had mentioned he was learning to code and write computer programs and that he was trying to start his own version of Craigslist, where people could list things for free (he never said what), and where other people would be able to purchase things (again, he never said what). In fact, even though he spoke about so many things, he never really said much of anything. It was sort of like talking to somebody who spoke in similes and there was always something hidden or left unsaid. Like the time I tried to call the number on his card when a bedroom light switch stopped working. A woman with an accent, not unlike his own, answered the phone and I asked if Boris was there and she said no. Then I asked if I had the right number for Boris the electrician and she said yes and hung up.

I tried again the next day and he answered and when he arrived,

I told him about the call. Without looking at me he said I must have had the wrong number. I laughed and said, "Oh, I thought it was your wife, you both have the same accent." He didn't seem to take this well and said sternly, "No. I am not married, it was nobody." I backed away and made myself busy in another part of the house. That's when our friendly chats sort of ended, but not my curiosity.

There was something not right, and for one of the first times in my life I felt like I did want to follow my gut. Something felt wrong, like really wrong, and I started to wonder about the woman who had answered his phone. I tried calling there a couple of times, with my number hidden, but it was just his voicemail and nobody ever picked up, but still, it nagged me. I tried to look up his Craigslist project and was redirected to some really weird places. Places I would not normally look at online: escort agencies and massage parlors, advertisements without addresses, just phone numbers. It was a whole part of life I was unfamiliar with and it made me even more curious, and more than a bit nervous, as to why these websites came up as associated with my electrician.

But I must not have felt any real peril for my life, unlike in the zombie dream I had where, once I knew I had the virus and that the change would happen any minute, I called and told everybody that I loved them, I hugged those who were close and felt a huge relief for being able to be free from the burden of things like mismanaging the bank account (a rather lovely feeling that made me happy to become one of the undead). And so, just nervous, but not in any real danger, I stepped forward and pushed myself into this person's life, even though my gut was now suggesting that I stop.

Here is where the last stupid thing comes in—I became obsessed with this guy. Or maybe, to be more specific, the fact that this guy was pushing me away made me want to know even more about him and to try even harder to find out his secrets. I am aware that this was a weird and perilous way of thinking, but that's how my mind works. Work for something and work hard at it and you will be rewarded with it no matter how bad it is for you on the scale of zero to ten, ten being the worst possible thing in the world. Boris was my ten.

Sometimes I feel like I go into things with such good intentions; maybe finding out Boris's secrets would lead both me and him to some sort of redemption and our slates would be wiped clean. Like that one time I thought I was being so helpful and proactive, but actually almost killed every living thing in my yard by doing what I believed was my part at saving the world, like so much depended on me and my actions. When I moved here to this house, I decided that not only would I try harder to "go green" and recycle more, I also decided that I would do my part to conserve as much water as I could, and this meant carrying buckets full of my bathwater out to the garden in order not to waste it. I had also read that Epsom salts were beneficial to your garden, so I felt even better knowing that I was helping the garden as well as watering it. After every bath, I made myself sweaty again by carrying bucket after bucket of water all around the yard. I went back to reading after everything in the garden began to wither and die and I learned that only a small amount of Epsom was beneficial; any more was toxic.

I had been killing my garden with kindness and good intentions, and that is how I have also gone about my relationships. When I stopped recycling the bathwater, things began coming back to life, and I finally put two and two together.

This is what happened with Boris the mystic Bulgarian: I put together Slavic-sounding women ("Not wife!"), unanswered calls and a seedy website, and this two-and-two, plus a few more weird details, led me to the conclusion that Boris was a trafficker, bringing eastern bloc girls into the country to marry Canadian men for money. Then I put myself in real danger when I mentioned this to a friend who worked at Immigration. Ephrem, former lover.

I laughed sitting nervously in his office that day and said he should put that on his name tag so people would know our connection. He didn't laugh back. Broken hearts are no joke, and I could see that he was struggling to remain polite; I had ghosted him before ghosting was fashionable or even had a name, ghosted like I realized he was too much Epsom salts. But here I was asking for a favor, and the only thing that kept him from throwing me out of his office was the fact that I was onto something. I had given him a piece of the puzzle he was working on and this was the big, huge middle piece.

Soon after my meeting with Ephrem, Boris showed up at the house having sort of figured out that it was me who had started the forward motion to have him charged and deported. The questions I would ask him as he tried to work; I have never been subtle. I felt nosey and I was. And like in the cop shows, where the prisoner escapes to seek a final revenge, Boris had snuck out of his apartment, which was being watched by the police, and had come to my house, waited for me outside, then forced his way in the front door and smashed me into a wall, the angry bulk of the man finally unleashing his size and the weight of his culpability just as the police entered, alerted by a neighbor. So that is my long-story-short except for some of the gory details you don't need to remember, like the broken arm and the really itchy cast.

For me this was the start of the grand reckoning which brings me here to this pen and this letter. A painful break, a realization and a rebuilding of not only my arm, but myself. I can still feel the gaze of the people in the Emergency waiting room staring at me—well, me and the wall behind me and I swiveled to look and see that I was sitting under a poster for domestic violence. I was the poster child and while I waited I slowly started to remember and recall and see patterns and shapes of people I had let, sometimes pulled, into my life.

After the episode with Boris, my countenance remained unchanged until the next day when I sat in the hot bath with my fresh cast wrapped in a garbage bag and began seeing my own patterns. There was a knock at the door and I stood up, wobbly from heat and awareness, put on my robe and stepped into the hall. I could see through the frosted glass the shape and colors of a police uniform and I shook red and dripping, like a birth, before I opened the door.

It was the officer who had been the "takedown" guy on the previous day. He was just calling in "to check if you're okay," and I could see his dimpled smile and a bit of a flash of fire in his eye. But here is when it happened, in that very moment I recognized him. I felt the fear in my gut and I listened. He handed me his card, said I could call his cell any time, but I handed it back to him with a polite "no thanks, I'm fine, all is well, thank you and goodbye," and shut the door on his surprised face. A face I knew would have had a flare of anger behind it at that moment, but I shut the door and went back to the tub to wash myself clean and be baptized.

So, as promised, I want to apologize to you, old me, old buddy, old pal. For mistakes I've made. I want to ask your forgiveness and repent from all of my grave errors in judgment, when I have injured this body instead of praising its strength, when I have tortured this mind instead of utilizing its capacity. I want to apologize now that I have outgrown my snakeskin and just want nothing more than to learn to love myself, rather than sit in a tub and unpack memories and hold grudges. I want to come clean.

And you're not alone here; I have a mountain of people to apologize to. All those other accumulated stupid things I've done, even though I was hyperaware of what I was doing and not listening to the warning screams from my gut, where instead I just kept advancing like so many soldiers at the front of some great war.

I don't know what I was trying to do, or who I thought I was trying to save, and so I'm sorry, from the bottom of my grubby four-year-old heart. And I promise you that I will stop now and try to live a quiet life, so that you don't have to show up at the door to your retirement with so much baggage in hand.

Signed me, at thirty-six.

Material Remains

Sarah Heath was an archaeologist by trait and by trade. When she was a child she loved to bury and dig up her dolls, her books and her mother's silverware. She would make up fantastic stories about the spoon she happened upon while on a dig in the back garden, giving an oration of the lost tribe's terrible history to her father's laughter and her patient mother's dismay.

Sarah Heath also liked rocks; they were solid and true. Her grandmother tells the story of when Sarah was three and used to walk in the garden, along the rock path, picking up small stones and hiding them in her mouth. When asked by her mother if she had any rocks, Sarah would put her hands behind her back and shake her head no, her cheeks as full as a squirrel. Her mother would search her little hands and then ask Sarah to open her mouth. "Spit them out," she would say, shaking her head and walking away, not seeing Sarah pick two back up, one going into her pocket and one back into her mouth, her small mind telling her already that she needed to be connected to something solid, and that even if it were not real food, she could pretend. That was back before she understood that the faded violets on her grandmother's windowsill were plastic and could not grow. The evolution of a lie.

As an adult, Sarah still played that archaeologist and rock-hound, often digging up painful memories carefully buried as a child, but only uncovering the top layer, removing just enough soil to reveal a glimmer of sharp, silver pain. Memories uncovered in this way would quickly be buried again until the next excavation, be it in the arms of another person used only for that purpose, or at her granny's kitchen table over a bowl of lemon gelato drizzled with yellow corn syrup, the sharp needing to be mixed with the sweet always.

As a working archaeologist, she loved nothing better than losing herself in a peat pit, stripping away centuries of someone else's memories frozen there in muddy time. This job gave her the peace she needed to keep her thoughts gentle and quiet, and nobody bothered her. She just did the work in a nondescript pit and drove back to her nondescript house in her nondescript car, where she could hide at the end of the day and lose herself in a book or bath or music and then just dream.

Her excavations fed her waking world, for as she worked she would carve out a story around a person to make the remains and artifacts her own. She would chisel at them and then gently brush away the sediment to reveal a friend, a husband, a child or a sibling and then create an entire world around them. She made connections that had never evolved naturally, that could never grow and last; like the violets they would sit and fade, remnants. But for the duration of the dig, those links felt solid and the stories real enough. Or at least, possible, and that was another shard closer to building a hopeful heart.

Sharp light woke Sarah on the morning of May 3. The freezing wind blew down from the north of Scotland and the sea churned a black that she could feel through the sheets and blankets she had tightly wrapped around her naked body. The old house groaned as if bemoaning the need to stand through yet another storm and the phone rang once, then stopped dead, and she knew the power was off. The wind chimes were clanging frantically against the side of the little red garden shed some fifty meters away, and fragments of light pierced swiftly moving clouds, adding a contrast of light and shade to the wings of the gulls that played on the wind.

An hour later, with her travel mug full of milky Ovaltine, Sarah walked out into the storm. She slung her backpack off her shoulder and onto the passenger seat, got into her car and then, through her rearview mirror, watched a newspaper being violently torn open and blown around the yard and into the street. She imagined herself as one of the pages, flying, tumbling and rejoicing in the dance, corners touching down—tap and rise, tap and rise—buoyant into the day, and she sighed at the joyful feeling that pushed from inside her chest wall and up into her neck, which tensed to squeeze that small happiness out.

As she pulled out of her driveway, the local radio station was reporting that a number of horses had been killed not far from her worksite. She shivered, except for her scar, which could no longer produce gooseflesh and so remained unmoved. Twenty minutes later, Sarah slowed down to look at the carnage. It was at a hairpin corner and the eight young foals lay bloody and piled on one side of the pavement. Sarah observed and concluded the road was slick, a lorry driver couldn't have stopped. The stud farmer who stood on the gravel shoulder looked ethereal through Sarah's foggy windshield as her wipers created a pair of wings for him. And in her mind she began to carve out his story: he was a good man, and she felt a warmth building in her as she thought about him coming home at the end of a workday, dancing her around the kitchen or surprising her at Christmas with something he had built by hand, or stunning her with his own poetry. But then as she drove closer, she saw him there on the roadside, sobbing with his head in his hands, his worn tweed jacket smeared dark red and a dirty flat cap on the ground beside him. She felt a heat break through her chest and tear apart her scar just a little bit and she realized that tears were streaming down her face too, steaming on the surface of her waxed jacket.

A small sob rose in Sarah's throat as she drove past the scene. Sometimes she needed a profound shock to make her synapses fire in the order necessary to reach down into the place where she was still one whole, moving person, and not the tattery bits that were stitched together so tightly they were immobile. Sarah turned off the radio and pushed a cassette tape into the old player and breathed out and gulped in the Gipsy Kings, the music connecting her to the place she wanted to be.

Around noon, tired of arguing with the blue tarp that would not stay tied down in the wind and memories that would not stay put, Sarah drove to the local pub for lunch. She caught a glimpse of herself in the mirror on the other side of the bar and did not recognize the woman who met her gaze. Her long dark hair was wet and windblown and stuck to her forehead. There was a splash of mud smeared on her face, made worse by the dirty hand which tried to rub it off, but mostly she was struck by the beauty the mirror gave her from a distance, and reflexively she stomped her foot sharply on the floor, which made the barman look in her direction. Sarah hovered in front of the mirror a moment longer before she walked to the back of the pub and into the washroom.

She folded a paper towel in half, wet it and cleaned her face. Then she paused and contemplated her reflection. Sarah was not one to spend time with mirrors, so when she did it was always a surprise. The age, another line, the solemn look that never faded even when she laughed, which was a rarity these past few years. Her cheeks and lips were ruddy and chapped from the elements, but it was her eyes that attracted people—they were dark, deep and sad, contrasted with the other colors of her face. Someone had once told her they could break your heart if you were not careful to look away. Sarah's body was not special, but was firm and strong and, when driven by her hard will, her strength belied her slight frame. She often ran a dig on her own and her superiors knew she could be counted on.

The strength, the eyes, the beauty—and then the big red splotchy scar that covered half of her face, most of her neck, and her left breast, where the skin always appeared thin and frail, even now, years after the hot wax had poured over her, her small, curious hand pulling the pan off the stovetop where her mother was making candles from their own beeswax.

In the pub's small bathroom she ran a red plastic comb through her tangled hair and thought about cutting it. It was more trouble than it was worth, but she did feel safe behind those locks. People would always notice the hair first and then the girl. It was safer that way. She always had something to stand behind.

"Which girl?" they would ask.

"That one there, with the long hair," would be the answer.

She sat over a steaming bowl of soup and let the heat warm her face. She glanced around. Two old men were arguing over football scores in the far corner, and the barman's wife and daughter were having a cup of tea with him at the bar, discussing the morning's accident, the two young granddaughters sitting at a nearby table playing Old Maid. The townspeople knew who Sarah was; it was she who kept them out of her world, never accepting an invitation, always with a handy excuse for not participating, making her work and home life more important than anything else. After a time they sensed her unwillingness and left her alone. Everyone was polite and pleasant though, and remained curious about the quiet woman, as she sat hunched at a corner table. Sarah concentrated on her soup, unaware.

There were days, fewer now that she was entering her fourth decade, when Sarah would put her hair up and apply makeup, just like her mother had shown her when she was thirteen, to cover the scar. She never left it on long—she didn't like the way it made her skin feel like a mask, but this was when men came to her, to that surprising beauty and the look of those dark eyes that pierced through their skin. In the beginning, she took any of them to her bed, amazed they would want to be with her. She didn't see what they were, hungry and dangerous, needing to save her in order to make themselves more powerful. These men would go from showering her with gifts and praise to threatening her and accusing her of being unfaithful when, her confidence approaching normal, she stopped to have a conversation with the cashier at the local grocers. Then a hand would come and slam her back down into uncertainty.

In the beginning, it was enough that they wanted her at all, and she squashed down any flare-gun warnings that fired into her mind, unwilling to listen, as she had listened to the laughter and smirks that had followed her down high-school hallways. In those beginnings with these men, she was cradled in the warmth of a fire that she could not build within herself, so instead she created fantastical stories about their pasts, their presents and their future together. But these bonfires just reheated the hot wax that had burned apart her left and right hemispheres, and Sarah felt no ownership over her split self. Her stories crumbled and fell, and parts of her always fell with them, leaving no trace in the ground.

Later, Sarah became a little more selective and searched for people that she thought could best take care of her. Some of these were people had good jobs and some seemed kind, at first, but underneath they were the same as the others—people who needed her to give them power over their own fear. One man slammed her into a wall, giving her a concussion. She had wanted to marry him.

They wanted to change her story and prove themselves the better writers, but they all lived the same lives, inside of grooves they could not circumvent, and so the narratives were always the same, no matter how hard she tried to revise the lines, and no matter how hard they pushed back.

Over the half-finished bowl of soup, Sarah's nose started to drip from the steam and the memories, and as she pulled a damp tissue from one of the many pockets of her cargo pants, her arm knocked her knapsack off the chair. When she picked it up she saw the Live Aloha! patch sewn on the side, an artifact from the past. A leftover memory of joy tried to bubble up, but she pressed it back down with the recollection of the truth of that particular trip, another relationship that had ended badly.

On her drive home, a Mini Cooper in front of her puffed exhaust that matched the blue of the Union Jack paint job that covered the car. She could just make out the top of a baseball cap in the front passenger seat that bobbed up and down as a boy sang along with the man behind the wheel—a father?—to something on the radio and Sarah smiled. She reached over and turned up her radio, trying to find the station and song to which the pair were singing.

Static and then The Beatles' "Penny Lane" played and in that moment the chorus made Sarah feel that she was part of the family in front of her as she saw the father? turn to the son? point his finger and deliver a do do do. Then Sarah was sitting in the car, and she was part of that family, heading home after a pizza night, and the man was looking into her eyes and mouthing I love you, and the boy was showing her a picture he had drawn of their family, all three in a row holding hands, and she felt a craving and a satisfaction all at once. Her skin felt the warmth of their breath and, within her story, she felt healed.

Sarah laughed aloud, but then old Mini turned left at the light and she was alone on the road and tired, having just lived an entire life in a few safe moments, and there was no echo of her laughter, just silence and the road in front of her.

Sarah often played this game as she drove, making imaginary friends and living stories with the people on sidewalks or in the cars that accompanied her on the road. Just in case, she thought. Just in case I had a flat, that sweet old Italian man in the red caravan would stop, he probably has tools in his boot that he carries everywhere. I'll bet he has kind eyes, I'll bet he likes to hold hands. Sarah could become a spouse, a sister, part of a family or a best friend with anyone in less than half a mile. Real life was awkward, she didn't know how to be or act, her skin did not stretch like that. It was safer to imagine a life, to keep a separation by degrees, through sediment or centuries. In the hazy distances she could reimagine herself in dozens of scenarios, without having to look at the reflection offered by clearer waters.

She pulled her car into the drive.

In her bath that evening, she watched a bath bomb effervesce and felt the tiny bubbles moving up her skin, like a tickle, or a soft touch, with no expectation. Small joy. And she looked out the window and saw the fading light and knew it was almost time. When she could see the branches of the beech tree dark against the sky, conducting the last rays of the sun's set, she felt her heart gallop. She rushed and slipped into her costume, carefully buckling her black shoes, and ran to the front door, clack, clack, clack, clack down the slate hall.

The door was made from a single, framed pane of glass and soon it would be dark enough to see her reflection in it. Here she would stand and wait, the anticipation and excitement creeping over and through her until at last she could witness her own sharp form standing opposite, and she could no longer see the dusty bag of tools on the floor beside the closet. Her hands rose and she began clapping, alternating hard and soft, fuertes and sordas, making her own music with the palmas, and began repeating the dance steps she had been learning, in tidy counts of twelve.

At the end of a long day a few weeks earlier, exhausted from building imaginary homes where she would never live, her mind had stopped and her mouse had clicked and she had followed an ad on the internet, randomly signing up for a series of free introductory dance classes after which her meaningless interior excavations stopped because, in this movement, she had found her own fire.

This dance was hers, just when she needed it most, and it asked nothing of her. The dance was hers and she slipped into it like a much-anticipated next bite of something delicious. It was another skin she could wear like a spacesuit—it connected her to her bodily functions, could breathe for her if needed, provided oxygen and sustenance; its rhythm providing a heartbeat and a way for her stiff skin to move naturally. The structure of the dance she used as bones and it held her up. The dress, her traje de flamenco, trussed her and then moved for her, where she could not. The ruffles floated and flowed and bounced and swept away the residuum of her excavations, leaving only joy.

The reflection of the woman in that night-paned glass, the one who returned her gaze, stood proudly, arms raised, and the pale light from the kitchen that shone on Sarah's scar revealed a rosy jewel.

This dance was hers and nobody else's. This dance was hers, and she came to it mightily.

Hollow Bones

Not having cream for my coffee was not an entirely new way to experience morning, but for some reason it made the memories flow hot and bitter today. The taste reminded me of being somewhere, but I couldn't put my finger on it. Somewhere hot, early in the day, maybe on the road after having slept on top of a picnic table at a roadside pullout. Or maybe at some cafe when I thought that coffee without cream would somehow be stronger and would shock my body awake, on one of the million road trips I took, sometimes to get away, sometimes because I had nowhere else to go, so comfort was found in the motion. Like when you rock a baby, and you are their home.

Early is the best time to be on the road, of course, that was in the olden days of travel, nowadays everybody knows that secret. Be up before the traffic, before the heat of the sun and before you are fully awake to the misery that your body, your very early morning body, presents you with—the shock of unfamiliar light and putting your feet to the floor, to carry the weight of you through another day. And when you were running, this weight of your body is compounded by the weight of your mind, and on some days is almost too heavy to bear. At least that's the way it was for me when I was fifteen and I also had to bear the weight of my chubby baby on my hip.

I was content to be on the road because I preferred to be moving. I was the momentum and I was in charge on my own pendulum's swing. Staying still meant looking at so many of my faults, the faults of who I was, the people I was with and the faults of the world (something I still have a very hard time with, especially now from where I sit in this later decade). Of course things were simpler back then, because I did not actually have to carry the weight of the world on my shoulders. I didn't know much but, being a ninety-eight pound weakling, I knew it was better that I didn't have to take on any more weight, or my knees might give out on me and I would be crushed by it all. And I couldn't afford to be crushed, my responsibilities were too great, so onto another Greyhound I would go. The "gray dog" we called it then and it was a huge step up from hopping a train or hitch-hiking, which was cold and dangerous and you needed two hands to hold a baby.

Like when the sun is too hot and you can feel the weight on you. Like when you hit the road a little later than you expected and the sun is already high and hot in the sky, and you curse your need for sleep and you drink your coffee black that day, for the pure jolt of it. The bitter roadside-cafe coffee with the soggy brown toast.

I've had so many of these mornings that now, looking back, I am surprised that I still love to travel. At the time they seemed trying I guess, not enough food or sleep, not enough money or resolve. Staying with people I didn't know and then didn't like when I did know them, out of necessity, but it always gave me something to write about, all of the interesting travel and work experiences.

The road gave me fodder for stories about painting silos, mucking stalls, cleaning houses, sleeping with insecure narcoleptic drug lords, looking after some family's screaming brood of youngsters, and the bleak, hot, dryness of a falling-down mansion, with an inhabitant so old I thought when she died the house would surely fall down with her and the whole thing would disintegrate in the heat of that sun that was so hot that even after supper we could not walk outside because the pavement burned our feet through our shoes.

And these experiences built up my bones when I didn't have enough food to eat. They built me up from the inside out like the delicately interwoven calcium labyrinth that is my frame. My arm bone is a trip back east where I saw a wall of headstones falling down a cliff into the sea, a pile of mistakes by the stonemason; my left femur is a tropical beach in the early morning where I sat and was almost killed by a rogue wave, and the vertebrae that make up my neck structure are snips of words that I read which were carved into the ceiling beam of an old barn, maybe only to be read by me, on that day: "August 1812—Had to bring in the hay early, big storm. Joseph and Hannah are wed." A diary of time and place, unmoving. All the while the experiences draw me to the same conclusion—I want to be still, and I want a home.

And where I go, she goes too, and so my daughter is built of mostly the same stuff, she breathed the same experiences of places that I did, the different airs. The airs of here's and there's. Blazing hot and frigidly cold. I wish I had the courage to ask her what she remembers, but in truth, I am afraid to know. I'm afraid to ask her fragile bird bones if they are truly hollow. I am afraid they'll break under the pressure of that question. As I sip my coffee, the strength of which has excavated these memories, I hope. I hope she can't remember all of the times on the road, but only recalls the sway and the movement of a train car and the feeling of flying.

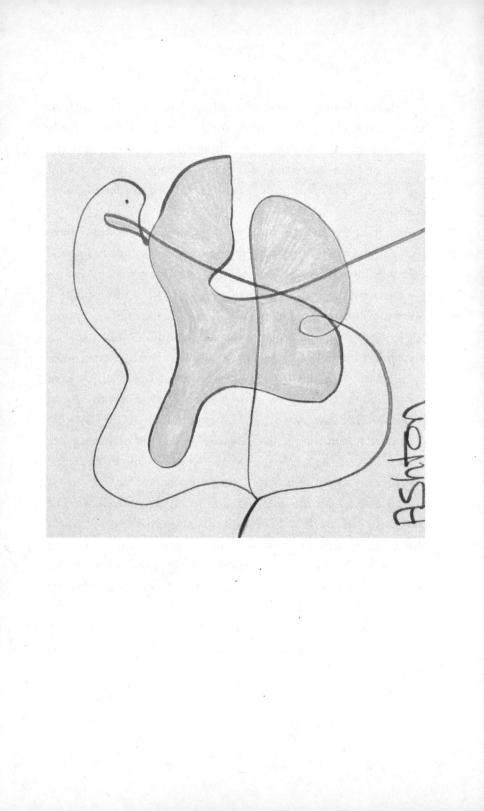

Mona Lisa

The tree coming through the roof was the end of the line for me. I had seen the workman working next door, and just as I was wondering what they were doing with the old cherry tree, the largest side of its double trunk smashed through the skylight. It lay neatly in front of my gas fireplace as if to keep warm. The next hours and days saw workmen and nails and wire and bits of glass everywhere, while the dog and I picked our way through the rubble.

Unbeknownst to the neighbors, who were footing the repair bill, the roof had started leaking around that skylight the other week and I had been wondering how I could afford to fix it. I'm thankful for small things.

And big decisions. The cherry tree crash made me realize that life is short, too short to worry about things and hate neighbors and bemoan shade trees. So, after my fifty-seventh birthday, I sold the house, which left me with enough cash in my bank account to see me through the rest of my days. I renewed my passport, handed my treasured pooch over to my daughter and left for Britain. I was officially "of no fixed address." Some would call that homeless, but I called it freedom, two things that look the same from the outside, both tidy two-syllable words, double e, double s, but different on the inside, one hollow, one full. It was a need like back in the day, when I needed to roam to fill my lonely heart, but the difference now is that it feels like staying still would be to wither and die; I need a new momentum to help push the air into and out of my lungs. I need different winds in my face. I think I am just built this way. When the pine cone is finished with the tree it drops and rolls away.

London

I had nobody to explain myself to. Just me in a part of the world that I had always wanted to explore, to live, to try, to test, and to see with my own eyes. Always the Anglophile, for years I had gorged on every British TV show, from baking to detective. I knew every bent copper, every best Bakewell tart. Wallowing in the deep bathtub in my hotel room in Earls Court, I felt untied, released from the iCal alarm beeping at me on the seventeenth of every month to pay the mortgage, no tax bill waiting for me every spring, no car to insure. I just lay there and smiled, every last invisible umbilical cord to my old life cut, tied off and tucked away to fall off once it had healed over.

When I was little, London meant fish and chips and the Queen of England, all revered and so fine she must have a gold toilet. Later it was Dickens sitting in a pub writing, and the Globe Theatre and Shakespeare's brilliant words. I didn't text my old student-friend-lover Jacob, who escaped here a decade ago and settled, which for him was a lot. But I did cruise his Instagram page and read his blog—one-way non-conversation seemed a comfortable way to bring that bit of the past with me.

Brighton

I used to loathe crowded buses when I had to take the Greyhound from place to place, ocean to ocean and town to town with a baby on my knee. But on this bus I had room. I was calm, looking at the fields and villages and rolling downs between London and Brighton. I have never seen fields as green or as tidy, surrounded by ancient rock walls and happy animals. To think I had been afraid I would miss the mountains and feel lost that my touchstones were no longer on the horizon. I had been afraid of so much, that I would sit and count my faults, feel all my guilt, but instead I only felt the movement under me, and gentle engine's roar, the vibration as we pulled away and were gone. Nothing to think about, just the sensation of weightlessness and being moved from one place to another, like my old pendulum days.

Now I had no plan but one goal: to see the Brighton pier in all shades of day, dawn to dusk, late night and in the middle of the night. I wanted to stand beside it in the water and look back at the town; my lungs needed to smell the air.

I had booked into Drakes, a rather nice hotel, because money was no longer a worry for me, and I could finally cast off that web of anxiety and savor every bite of food I put into my hungry mouth without questioning where the next meal would come from, or what I would have to do for that baker in order to hold that warm bap in my hand.

I walked through the Lanes, antiques and bric-a-brac and tat. I paid by debit, a tap here and there. I didn't buy the things I used to, things that kept me safe and made me comfortable, back when I didn't know what comfortable was. Later, in the second bathtub of my trip, I allowed myself to soak into the new feeling of being unburdened by dollars, recollecting all the times when it was exactly the opposite. Begging for a roof, room or food. I stayed there briefly, just touching on the memory long enough, the memory of walking up rickety blue back stairs, to knock on the door, crying to the elderly neighbors, asking for a bit of bread and milk.

"We don't have much ourselves you see," they said, handing me half a crusty brown loaf and a glass jug half full of milk. It made me cry even harder, the look in their eyes. So much bad feeling in that dirty little town. Such a hard life for a kid. Me and mine.

I repacked that memory like folding an old letter from a lover, tucking it into a book and lying back to listen to the sounds of the pier at dusk through the opened window on the balcony of my little room in the quaint whitewashed hotel.

Wandering downstairs for breakfast delighted me, everything delighted me: fresh hot coffee, matching white china, flaky pastries that make me wonder at the hands that had been up all night preparing them, the love that went into them.

And the joy of unfolding a new map on the starched white tablecloth where, with a scented green marker I'd brought with me, I added dots to places on the map that I want to see, following the spearmint smell from point to point. Some names were familiar because I had read about them from various sofas and chairs in my other life, others made my gut ping when I read the syllables: Winchester, Poole, Exeter, Torquay, Bristol, Bath, Swindon, Tintagel, Gloucester.

On childhood trips, I was made to feel bad for not spending every minute out exploring and living every single second of where I was, trying this or that, doing whatever thing needed to be seen at wherever place we were at. At Disneyland, every ride, every sight, every taste and noise all had to be packed into a day or a miserable week, because we were only there as tourists and so had to use up all of our tourist points, all of our tokens to get as much in as possible—photos and souvenirs—so we could look back and show off to whomever we could.

No more. No more.

An email from home: It feels like you're missing. Subtext: You are shirking your responsibilities. What responsibilities I couldn't quite figure out. I was no longer a homeowner; I was a grandparent and dog owner, but that's it. I didn't owe money or favors, and the only thing I was missing was my dog. I Skyped with her every few days. I didn't know if she could see me, but I could see her and she could at least hear my voice.

Pontypridd

I watched a show about Saxons and Danes once and, in the program, they pronounced Wales as two syllables, Way-lez, and since then that's how I've said it in my mind. My maternal grandmother's family was from here, Pontypridd, and the house is still standing I was told. I did want to see that, and maybe to go inside to see what I would feel like standing there. My brother and I did that once before, visited the house we grew up in, and the woman at the door, though surprised, did let us in and gave us a tour around. She was very kind, and everything was so small. My bedroom where I used to stand at the foot of my bed and recite my thank-you speech for the Nobel prize for writing or curing something, that room with the ladybug wallpaper where I built big dreams, and where I was also broken-hearted that my dog had to live in a cold kennel in the basement. That's where the crack in my heart started and it just grew from there. But now I used the handy, tiny sewing kits from each hotel room I stayed in to put it back together, stitching tidy rows now that my hands were patient and

I had time and I was repatriated. Some spots I left frayed because they looked more interesting and I liked the texture, like the lines on my face now. Road maps of where I've been.

I was floating, another big hotel bathtub. I liked the body I was in now and to prove just how much, I'd stopped shaving my legs, wearing make-up and coloring my hair. This was how I celebrated me, not just by coloring outside the lines, but by erasing the lines altogether. I no longer cared how people looked at me, I felt no guilt for the way I look. I was living outside in, in such a pure way.

People could look at me however they liked, but nothing they thought about me could be worse than the labels I had given myself in the past. Now I dropped them here and there as I went— there goes selfishness, dropped into the cold sea with the spray in my face. I saw it float away and become seafoam and it looked green and healthy.

The front desk called to check in on me around 11:00 a.m. and when I told them I was sick they sent up a tray that would have been fit for a fine lady in Georgian times: cream scones, a pot of tea and bowl of strawberries and some sort of eggy omelet thing that I couldn't quite bring myself to look at right away. A fever had set in, as it often does when traveling, new airs and germs, and I took a cup of tea and honey back to my bed, where I stayed for a day and a half until I felt well enough to "take the air" again, and I bundled up and took a slow meander down the high street.

When I got back shivering to my room, I implemented the rash new plan that had come to me, one to fully shed my old life. I suddenly wanted to see me how others see me, I craved being naked in front of people as I was, not as how I thought I should be, the way I had for so many years. I was not here to please anybody, and I thought of all the things I'd done for men and sex and women

180

and sex and I knew in my bones that I needed to do this one last thing to shed my old life. I began an internet search for "art schools Wales" and sent several emails, applying to be a life model.

I wanted to be seen, I wanted to be inspected, I wanted them to see me, and these fifty-seven years, how they look on me. I wanted to stand, or preferably lie, on a slab or carpet and have students draw every bit of me in their way. I wanted to be stripped of my own emotion and be given their interpretations to try on.

And so I lay in bed, chesty and coughing, waiting for a response. I didn't have to wait long—apparently age was "in"—and many people wanted to use me in this way. I booked the first sitting for four days later, when I should be over my cold. I thought of all the times I disliked having my photo taken, mainly because when I was young it meant getting my hair cut in some weird way that I hated. It meant smiling at a strange man whom I felt afraid of, whose camera ordered me to "act in a way that is not natural and I will snap you in that pose." I hated posing, posing was not my life and I spent the rest of my time doing the opposite, so I would never be caught in that pose, those poses, ever again.

Four days later, I couldn't wait to rip my clothes off. I mumbled and unbuttoned like my shirt was on fire, wheredoyouwantme? and I was excited and flushed and my heart was racing. I wondered what the fifteen artists would make of me. Of this form of me. Baggy and flustered. Pink and mottled.

I lay back on a raised dais about twenty-four inches off the ground and covered with a yellow, slippery sheet. I thought it might be cotton sateen, a high thread count. The instructor suggested I make my arms comfortable, over my head, but my shoulders would not work like that so they lay by my side. I put one foot on the floor, a knee raised and you could see my underneath bits, but I didn't mind and the cool air on me felt good. I knew I had a Mona Lisa smile, I could feel it there, and I wondered if Mona Lisa posed for Leonardo without her pants on. Then I fell asleep on the plinth to the sound of charcoal on rough-tooth paper and paintbrushes clinking in jugs of water and mineral spirits and there was no other human sound. I could have been anywhere.

When I woke up from my dozing, I felt my skin prickle with the realization of where I was. I shivered and I knew that every part of me was now "up," north as she goes: goose bumps from the sudden shiver of realization; nipples (I hated the word) from their shock at being in an open space, uncovered and revealed, unburdened by padded nylon and elastic contraptions used to disguise their existence; the hair on my arms and the back of my neck; my heightened nerves and the bit of my breakfast that threatened to come up even higher as every bit of me tensed in expectation, waiting, but for what, a climax of some sort? Bent coppers to run in and arrest somebody? Some sort of medical emergency? I tensed for a minute, but then relaxed back into it, letting my mind drift again, knowing I was out of that old life. There was no need now for my heart to beat above its comfortable resting pace, and I knew there was nothing I needed to hide, and nowhere to hide, even if I wanted to, the yellow sheet having slipped off some time ago. I didn't need to hide, ever again—I raised a flag on all of my peaks and conquered an undiscovered country.

I imagined them all touching me, I could feel their gazing, the intensity of their looks, deciphering my angles as I did the same from my supine position. It gives you a lot of time to think, being unable to move, being in this different sort of pose, but not a pose. I tried to imagine what it would like to be strapped into the electric chair, or on the table before the lethal injection. All eyes, all judging eyes on you, the only difference was here they didn't know my crimes and I was reduced to an object. So, even though I had come here to be seen, I was not. I was only my body and they had no attachment other than to the page in their sketchbooks and portfolios, and though some would pen my name beside or on the back of the paper, most would give me a number, or another title: Female, 57. The most insignificant label, and the most significant of my life, all in one.

Skegness

Three other studios wanted to book me, but I sent my apologies and moved on to Skegness. I wanted to feel the North Sea air. I was wind and, as the old saying goes, just went wherever it blew me. I used to attribute that old saying to people who were "shirking their duties," although when I thought about it, I didn't even know what that meant. I remembered it was said to me by people I loved, who didn't want to love me back.

The boardwalk lost my interest, and on the way back to my hotel, I passed a bakery and a new craving filled me—fresh bread. I stood in the line outside the old brick building and I practically threw my money over the shoulders of the others there. When they handed me the loaf, I squeezed it too hard, but it sprang back and I was elated. I remembered over forty years ago: "Don't hug the baby too hard, it's fragile." I hugged the warm loaf a little too close to me again and didn't care. It was warm and perfumed and I imagined I could feel its heartbeat, like I could feel mine when I lay on the cold plinth. I couldn't wait until I got back in my room; I pinched off a hunk in the elevator and chewed it slowly as I walked to my room.

I sent out emails again, offering to pose at whatever art studio on the South Coast would take me.

Poole

Room service, which turned out to be the owner's teenage son, brought me a pot of tea and scones, this time with soft Devon clotted cream on the side and I realized that maybe I was living one of those books where a foodie travels across Europe, gorging on everything local. The UK was feeding me like an infant, the new person I was, naked and craving and I needed to see myself that way.

The first time I looked, the students were each still standing beside their work as I was shown around. Some shook my hand, some smiled and some ignored me, like I was an un-person and just the object that must remain an object. I remembered the feeling of seeing myself. It was not like looking in a mirror, well maybe it was, but through somebody else's eyes. I could recognize parts of myself in each picture.

In the next studio, the owner let me come back after the students had gone. I walked around the easels, really looking, for the first time at leisure, at so many MEs. I was so many different people. I was a different person to each artist, and so I must be to everybody I have met. That's a lot of faces, but I no longer felt the weight of their gaze, my bones were built and solid now and, in this later decade, were more likely to lose a little of themselves. The bits I left in the portraits, the bits I willingly gave away.

No wonder I was always so tired in my younger years. I looked at the different parts of me and how they put me together. The views were as different as each artist, and I marveled at how I had tried all my life to please so many people, when each person's experience of me was so different.

A slaughter.

A symphony.

184

Acknowledgments

Thanks to The Writer's Studio at Simon Fraser University, my mentor Stella Harvey and my cohort Purnima, Joanna, Montana, Jeff, Karen, Heige, Beth, Debbie and Isabella, for early feedback and championing many of these stories.

To William W. Campbell, MD who provided information and clarification, to Aisling and my early readers for your keen eyes, to all of my friends and family, to every dog I've loved who kept me company as I wrote, and for the many rejections that I have received over my lifetime that have kept me moving forward, I am so grateful.

About the author

Jenn Ashton is an award-winning visual artist and the author of the prize-winning "Siamelaht" in *British Columbia History Magazine* and the recipient of the Muriel's Journey Prize for Poetry, both in 2019. *People Like Frank* is her first collection of short fiction, where she writes from her broad range of experiences with health and social issues.

Jenn is a graduate of Simon Fraser University (Criminology, Biomedical Physiology and Kinesiology and The Writer's Studio). She lives in North Vancouver, B.C. Learn more at JenniferAshton.ca.